NOTICE

The following pages contains adult content and have been written and shared for entertainment purposes only.

The 'manual' below is a product of fiction, and written only for the purposes of fantasy. No one should take anything written in this manual as actual advice or a recommendation to partake in any behavior of any kind.

All individuals referenced below are fictional characters over the age of 18. All activities referenced or described below are between consenting adults in a consensual, BDSM setting.

As a friendly reminder, any actual engagement with BDSM fantasy play in the real world should always be done with the full consent and awareness of all parties involved.

CONTENTS

The Miracle of Diaper Domination   vii

PART I
REGRESSION TECHNIQUES

1. Bathroom Regulations   3
2. Underwear Inspections   6
3. Induced Bed Wetting   8
4. Night Diapers   11
5. Toilet Training   14
6. From Pull-Ups to Pampers   16
7. If All Else Fails   19

PART II
BACK TO BABYHOOD

8. The Power of a Pair of Scissors   25
9. Picking New Names   27
10. Buying Diapers   29
11. Diaper Checks   32
12. Embracing Messy Diapers   34
13. How to Change a submissive's Diaper   38
14. Pubic Hair   41
15. Baby Wardrobe   42
16. The New Nursery   44
17. Feeding   47
18. Taking Temperatures   50
19. Toys   51
20. Other Activities   53

PART III
RULES FOR LITTLES

21. Example Rules List   59

PART IV
TRADITIONAL DISCIPLINE

22. Time-Out	63
23. Spanking	66
24. Writing Lines	70
25. Bedroom Door Removal	72
26. Holding Their Tongue	73
27. Mouth Soaping	74
28. Chores	76
29. Earlier Bedtimes	78
30. Delayed Diaper Changes	80
31. Crawling	82
32. Reducing Their Age	83
33. Sent Outside	86
34. Headphones	87
35. Journaling	88
36. Castor Oil	90
37. The Punishment Wheel	92
38. Rewards	93

PART V
HUMILIATION

39. Use Your Words	97
40. Public Outings	99
41. Throw a Party	101
42. Diaper Disposal	104
43. The Potty Song	105
44. Starting a Blog	107
45. Writing on Diapers	109
46. The Big Shave	110
47. Penis Humiliation	112
48. Hiring a Baby Sitter	114
49. Schedule a Doctor's Visit	116

PART VI
RESTRAINTS & BONDAGE

50. Diaper Tape	121
51. Adding Bulk	122
52. Restraints on the Changing Table	123
53. Sight and Sound	125

54. Keeping Hands Out and Diapers On	127
55. Restrictive Mittens	129
56. Locking Plastic Pants	131
57. Locking Pajamas	133
58. Other Articles to Secure Diapers	135
59. Crib Restraints	137
60. Leashes and Harnesses	139
61. Adult Baby Stroller	140
62. The Bouncy Seat	142
63. Straightjackets	143
64. Pacifier Gags	144
65. Pacifier Feeder	146
66. Learning to Crawl	147
67. Wrapped in Plaster	149

PART VII
SISSIFICATION

68. Sissy Catalysts	153
69. Sissy Names	155
70. Sissy Wardrobe	156
71. Inside the Diaper	158

PART VIII
SEX

72. Bottom Inspections	161
73. Masturbation	164
74. Masturbation Part II	169
75. Edging	171
76. Chastity	173
77. Prostate Massage	174
78. Vibrators	177
79. Pegging	179
80. Teaching Little's How to Give	180
81. Cuckolding	182

PART IX
FORCED INCONTINENCE & ADVANCED DIAPER USAGE

82. Catheters	187
83. Laxatives - A Primer	189

84. Enemas	192
85. Hollow Butt Plugs	194
86. Anal Stretching	196
87. Constipation	198
88. The Banana Technique	199
89. Marshmallows	202

PART X
ENHANCED PUNISHMENT

90. Ice	207
91. Diaper Rash	208
92. Diaper Withdrawal	210
93. Itchy Diapers	212
94. Chafing Velcro	213
95. Clothespins	214
96. Spicy Foods	216
97. The 'Time-Out' Pillory	217
98. Dildo Stool	219
99. Figging	221
100. A Whiff of their Own Medicine	223
101. The Reverse Diaper Change	224
In Conclusion	226
More from Nanny Chloe	227

THE MIRACLE OF DIAPER DOMINATION

As a dominant woman, there is nothing more pleasing to me than the process of regressing adult submissives back to diapers.

My eyes (and my groin) savor every chance I get to watch someone who formerly prized themselves on their independence, maturity, and adulthood, be forced to wear diapers 24/7, dress like a toddler, and depend on their caretaker for their most intimate needs.

But why is Diaper Domination so effective?

The first and most basic answer to this question is that toilet training is a cornerstone to the psychological development of every human being. There is no need more universal than the need to relieve one's bladder or bowels. Having one's basic toileting needs converted into the humiliating act of using a diaper and relying on a caretaker to change them out of their mess is an exquisite tool of domination in of itself.

As a caretaker, I have learned to revel in the sight of one of my submissives quietly going into the corner after lunch to 'do their business'. Watching them reckon with the fact that they no longer have basic privacy in regards to their toileting, let alone the infantile sensation and humiliating smell that follows their primal act, gives me an enormous thrill and surge of power.

But the second answer goes beyond the simple (yet profound) act of requiring the submissive to use diapers for their toileting needs.

I believe that successful diaper domination also entails regressing the submissive back to so many other wonderful aspects of toddlerhood — from being confined in a crib, to nursing with nanny, to wearing clothes that amplify and celebrate the submissive's newly diapered state.

Therefore, while 'Diaper Domination' is a useful shorthand, a more full title for the method described in this guide might be 'Adult-Baby Transformation' or 'Psychological Diaper Regression.'

Let me expand further by giving an example.

Imagine dealing with a disrespectful adult male housemate who consistently failed to clean up after themselves, played their music too loud late at night, and generally treated you with a very rude and disrespectful attitude.

Now imagine said rude housemate after you've successfully submitted them to your authority by means of the diaper domination method.

In the place of arrogance and rudeness, you would have sweet baby talk and laughter.

In the place of their laziness and taking you for granted, you would have an obedient boy who did all the chores you required him to do lest he face strict punishment.

And in the place of a man's terrible hygiene and etiquette in your house's bathroom, you would now have complete control over all of their bodily functions (and your bathroom back). You would totally determine their state of cleanliness as you changed their diapers while they held their hands above their head and sucked their paci, grateful to be under your complete control.

That's because the process of diaper domination is a process of *psychological transformation*. The material tools and techniques of diaper domination are designed to do far more than regress your submissive in *appearance*, (although it does make them *adorable*, I must say!). It regresses their *whole being* to a psychological development stage they thought they long ago left behind.

I believe diaper domination is magical, not just because it changes submissive's *behavior*. It also transforms their *mental and emotional age* to whatever you would like it to be.

I wrote the following guide because I wanted to give other caretakers the tools, techniques and tips I've discovered through my years of hard work dominating submissives with diaper domination and age regression.

Throughout this guide, I give personal examples from both my own experience and the experience of other domme's I know.

Some of the men and women submissives listed in this guide were ABDL diaper lovers and fetishists. Many were not though, as I and many of the other domme's I know derive the most joy from subjecting totally unsuspecting submissives into a world of diaper domination that they never could have seen coming.

Enjoy!

PART I
REGRESSION TECHNIQUES
GETTING SUBMISSIVES INTO DIAPERS

The first step to successful Diaper Domination is how you get your submissive to start wearing diapers. As you'll see from the techniques below, you should embrace the idea of a *process*.

To explain, let me refer to the tale of the boiling frog. It's well known that if you wish to boil a frog for dinner, if you drop said frog into water on your stove that is already boiling, they will immediately leap out of your pot and cause a great mess.

However, if you place the frog into the water while the water is cool, then begin to gradually heat the water, the change will be too incremental for the frog to notice. He'll soon relax into passivity as the water boils around him.

With apologies to our little frog friend, this is to say that if you advance diapers on your submissive incrementally, they'll have less chance to object, or even notice, their process of regression. This makes the potential for their successful domination that much greater.

That being said, sometimes dominants don't always have the fortune of plans succeeding exactly as planned. The dominant should always be ready and willing to improvise, with the end goal of a diapered submissive always in sight.

1
BATHROOM REGULATIONS

The first rule to impose on your not-yet-diapered submissive is regulations around their bathroom usage.

Possible catalysts for imposing such rules are plentiful. For example, I know a house keeper who rented a room to a boy she targeted for submission. One day, when she found droplets of urine on the seat of the toilet, she put a lock on the door, and insisted that he ask her for permission to use her bathroom from now on, as she could no longer trust him capable of keeping it clean without her present.

So, for example, you might require that they must now ask you for permission before using the toilet. Have them come to you and explain that they have to "go." Then, respond in such a way to maximize their humiliation.

"You have to go where?" You might reply.

"To the bathroom," they would say.

"To do what?" You would press again.

"To go pee," they would reply again.

"You don't have to go poop? Because I need to know if you're going poop so I can check the toilet when you're finished," you would reply again.

You can imagine the shade of red the submissive's cheeks would start to burn at this line of questioning. The key is to force them into the position of explaining their bathroom habits to you, and to any eavesdropping bystanders, in detail.

Further, as you've accustomed them to requiring your permission to relieve themselves, you can then slowly introduce the phenomenon of denial.

"Sorry, I'm busy right now, you're going to have to wait until I finished with this," you might reply, forcing them to hold their bladder and do the potty dance as they wait for you.

Another method I know some domme's enjoy deploying is instituting specific times of day their submissives are allowed to use the bathroom. Say 8am, 12pm, 4pm, and 9pm. The excuse the domme provides is that the submissive is now a terrible burden on her time, and the domme needs to keep the sub's breaks to regular intervals for efficiency reasons.

If the submissive sleeps in past 8am? Then they lose their morning bathroom time. If they choose to stay up late instead of going to sleep at a reasonable time, and then have to use the bathroom late at night? Well too bad again.

Needless to say, such a regimen will likely result in some sort of potty accident for the submissive sooner rather than later, giving the dominant the chance they need to impose a diaper requirement on the submissive.

∼

ANOTHER LAYER of humiliation a dominant might enjoy is subjecting said dominant to supervised bathroom use during the imposition of the above bathroom regulations.

After all, if the dominant say, leaves drops of urine on the toilet seat or perhaps forgets to flush their waste, they clearly require help during their eliminations.

If you wish to go a different direction than the above-mentioned permission/scheduled toileting process, you might remove the door to the sub's bathroom altogether. Knowing that they are now subject to your view any time they wish to use the bathroom might be humiliation enough for your purposes.

Many submissives will find it difficult to eliminate their urine at all while being supervised. As a domme, you can use this to your advantage.

"Oh, so you were lying about needing to use the bathroom just because you wanted to waste my time?" You might scold them. "Well why don't we take away your bathroom privileges for a few hours so you can understand the value of using my bathroom," you might say, imposing a sentence on them that will surely make them squirm.

You might also, as a domme, start to require that you be the one who wipes for your submissive when they're finished with their elimination. It won't be hard to come up with a reason for why you insist they need your help (the next chapter deals specifically with soiled panties and skid marks), and they will hardly have experienced anything more humiliating than having their domme wipe their poopy bottom like they were still in toilet training.

Further, subjecting your domme to such intimate handling and wiping down there, as well as eagle-eyed supervision during their toileting process, will make their transition to diaper changes by your hands that much more seamless.

2

UNDERWEAR INSPECTIONS

I am yet to encounter an unruly boy who does not frequently leave skid marks in his underwear at the end of the day. (Personally, I'm of the believe that this enough is proof that almost all men belong in diapers. But that's beside the point.)

For women, it's less common, but other varieties of stains in their underpants can give you the same sought-after leverage.

One way I've approached this in the past is that I'll gradually start doing laundry for the submissive as a favor. submissives, typically being the lazy and undisciplined type already, always gladly accept my offer.

Then, one day I'll sit them down at the kitchen table, and suddenly display several of their underwear inside out on the table for them look at.

"Can you explain to me what these stains are?" I'll ask in an authoritative tone as I point to the clear skid marks on their underwear.

Typically, they'll stammer a response along the lines of, "I don't know."

"You don't know?" I'll reply sharply. "That's even worse. That means your problem is so bad, you're not even capable of understanding what you did in your underpants."

Their face will burn hot red, and usually they'll try to provide a satisfactory answer. "I guess I didn't wipe good enough," they'll mutter.

And that's when you have all the leverage you need. Using their own words against them, you can simple repeat, "You didn't wipe good enough, remember?" as you impose the bathroom regulations explained above on them. After all, how could they argue with their own admission of inadequate bathroom hygiene? Or the evidence of their underwear splayed out right before their eyes?

In addition to supervised toileting, I've also imposed nightly underwear inspections of the submissive's underwear to make sure they didn't have any messy 'accidents' during the day. Oh, what fun it is to wave a submissive's briefs in their face as you point out their dirty stains. The humiliation in their eyes is truly priceless!

That being said, I feel compelled to share one personal anecdote regarding this method. I once worked with a submissive who was in fact, highly fastidious about their bathroom hygiene. Much to my disappointment, I never once discovered a wayward stain in their underpants.

After weeks of frustration about this fact, do you know what I did? I simply used a melted bar of chocolate to create the stains in their underpants artificially! The submissive had no idea that the stains were fake, and what's more, it was precisely his pride in his fastidiousness that made him all the more mortified when I confronted him about his problem! To my delight, his greater humiliation only gave me more leverage to impose my regressing regulations.

Was I dishonest? Yes. But the way I look at it, we domme's know what's best for our submissives, and we owe it to them to return them to diapers by all means necessary.

3

INDUCED BED WETTING

The easiest and most successful way to get your submissive to start wearing diapers is for your submissive to start wetting the bed.

That being said, cases of an adult submissive actually wetting the bed spontaneously and without your interference are quite rare. Bed wetting is accurately understood to be a problem that primarily exists for adolescents, and it's highly unusual for an adult to suddenly begin releasing their urine while they sleep unless there's a very clear underlying medical issue.

But you don't have to let your submissive know that. And there are a few tools I've employed to encourage the desired, bed-wetting outcome, which I'll explain below.

That being said, one exception I've found is those under the influence of alcohol (typically men).

Personally, I think alcohol is a nasty habit for any submissive, and the first time I learn of a perspective submissive's drinking habits, I look forward to their regression even more so I can soon stop worrying about them damaging themselves in that way.

But it's also the case that when adults fall asleep after a serious night of binge drinking, about 10% of them will release their urine during their sleep. This is worth keeping in mind, because should your submissive return home highly intoxicated, you should be prepared to take advantage of any accidents they have first thing in the morning.

But short of alcohol intoxication, most submissives are going to need your 'help' wetting the bed.

The first technique is to plant artificial urine in their bed while they're in a deep sleep. I know some domme's that have gotten away with just using warm water and a turkey baster to 'plant' the 'urine' on their submissive before they wake.

However, I'm highly suspicious of this method, as water does not smell like urine, and it seems that the submissive would recognize this pretty easily.

Where this method does seem to make sense to me though, is in the cases where the application of warm water to your submissive's crotch while they're sleeping stimulates their actual desire to release their urine. This can be done by aiming the application of warm water to the submissive's perineum, which is the area of flesh between the genitals and the anus. Rinsing this area with water has been shown to induce urination in medical settings. Thus, if done properly, a 'fake' accident can quickly become a real one.

An alternative to just plain warm water would be a fluid like warm, slightly watered down apple juice. For an unsuspecting submissive who has no reason to be suspicious of why their pajamas are wet, the strange smell and stickiness of the substance is typically enough to convince them they wet themselves.

I know another domme who insists on the real thing. She'll either collect her own urine, or collect her submissive's urine from the toilet bowl without them knowing. Then, she'll warm it up and deposit it on the submissive's crotch by the same method above while they sleep.

The unfortunate risk any domme runs for both of the above-mentioned methods is the risk of getting caught during the depositing of the 'accident', so to speak, should the submissive suddenly wake up.

Any domme worth her salt should be dexterous enough to hide any incriminating implements through sleight of hand before being confronted. Similarly, they should be able convince a submissive that their memory of them standing in their room in the middle of the night was clearly a dream — one that indicated their subconscious yearned for said dominant to have more control over their life.

That being said, neither of those situations is ideal, and so the other method here involves the purposeful inducing of bedwetting on behalf of the submissive with less risk of getting caught.

I know one Dominant, a nurse by trade, who insists that their submissive drink warm milk that she prepared, 'to help them sleep,' given 'all the getting up they do in the middle of the night.'

The warm milk, of course, will most certainly help them sleep, as unbeknownst do the submissive, this Dominant will have spiked the milk with the appropriate sleeping medications and muscle relaxants necessary to induce bed wetting. (Note: It is never okay and may be very dangerous to give anyone medications without their knowledge and consent.)

But even without the help of specific medications, a large glass of warm milk right before bed, combined with the bathroom access restrictions discussed above, will likely result in some sort of night time 'accident' in due time.

4

NIGHT DIAPERS

Once you've 'busted' your target submissive for wetting the bed, it's quite easy to insist they begin to wear 'protection' in for the form of GoodNites pull up diapers, or another form of 'night time protection'.

Of course, most submissives will immediately balk at such a notion, but it's not hard to win this argument. The fact that they've ruined their bedsheets, or that they require you to do extra laundry, or concerns about their hygiene and safety are all valid reasons to demand they begin to wear night diapers.

I know of a domme who had her current live-in boyfriend as the target of her regression and domination. For her, it was very easy to demand that if her boyfriend wanted to continue sleeping in the same bed with her, that he had to wear protection, as she had every right to sleep without expecting to get peed on! Her boyfriend's humiliation and desire to continue sleeping in the bed with her swiftly convinced him to comply with her demands. (He had no idea that it was precisely his girlfriend who was behind his 'bedwetting' in the first place!)

I believe the greatest chance of success with this stage relies on you buying the night time diapers for your submissive without their knowledge, and springing it upon them right before bedtime. They'll be least likely to argue you with you if they're tired and just want to go to bed, and will probably put the diaper on just to make you go away and allow them to go to sleep.

It's important that you closely supervise the submissive as they put their night time diaper on, and I highly recommend you stick your fingers into their diaper, to 'check' the fit. They will feel very humiliated having you supervise them and probe them in such a way, and it lays the ground work for future diaper checks of this nature.

It's recommended that you continue to induce night-wetting for the submissive in their new night-time diapers as many days as possible in the following week.

I like to buy a large, monthly calendar featuring babyish, pink and blue cartoons and hang it in my submissive's bedroom as their 'accident calendar.' I then make a deal with them that if they can stay dry for a certain amount of days (say, every day for one week), that I'll let them sleep in their 'big boy underwear' again.

This technique is great fun because it positions me, as the domme, to seem very reasonable about my expectations and goals. It manipulates the submissive into blaming themselves when they inevitably fail to stay dry the required amount of days. (Sometimes I like to let them go six days without an accident, then induce an accident on the seventh day to heighten their feeling of embarrassment and frustration.)

I recommend always checking the submissive's diaper before they wake up by means of sticking your hand into their diaper, which involves brushing your hand against their genitals. Not only will the experience of waking up with their domme 'inspecting' their privates be highly embarrassing, but combined with the fact that they will be in a diaper soaked with their pee, their morning's will soon become a routine experience of deep humiliation and submission.

I usually let my submissives change out of their wet diapers themselves for their first few days, but then one night I'll notice 'diaper rash' on them, and insist they've been failing to clean themselves properly in the morning.

From then on forth, I will insist that when they wake up in wet diaper, that they lay on their bed and put their legs up as I un-tape their diaper and clean them up with baby wipes.

When you've gotten this far with your submissive, it's not long until they'll be wearing real diapers full time.

5

TOILET TRAINING

Another method I wish to mention in this section involves specifics inspired by toilet training methods for toddlers. The way to think about this is that since your submissive is clearly incapable of handling their toileting (see above), you will need to subject them to a course of formal 'potty training'. Of course, little do they know, you'll really be subjecting them to a sort of 'reverse potty training.'

This can work well combined with the methods described above regarding restricted bathroom usage. You can tell your submissive that because they're having accidents, at night or otherwise, you need to force them to 'practice' holding it.

Now, when you arbitrarily take away their chance to use the bathroom, or require that they wait say, another twenty minutes, they will internalize their humiliation and uncomfortableness as *their* shortcoming, as *their* infantile inability to hold it.

Another technique involves the use of a kitchen timer. You can either force them to sit on the potty for a full fifteen minutes whenever they go to the bathroom, "To make sure everything is really drained," an uncomfortable and humiliating amount of time for your submissive to be naked on the toilet in front of you.

Or you can do the opposite, and restrict the amount of time in the bathroom to an arbitrarily short duration. (Imagine needing to defecate, and only getting 60 seconds to finish and wipe before you domme pulls your pants up on you.)

I've also seen splendid use of a children's 'training potty' displayed out in the living room, or even the kitchen.

You might introduce such a children's potty by explaining, "I can tell you're having issues with the big kid toilet. I lot of immature girls like yourself can feel intimidated or anxious to use a toilet so big, so I got you this adorable children's potty to go in instead."

Or, you might simply explain that since they made a mess on the lid of the 'big potty', they now need to use a potty 'more suited for their age.'

Both the uncomfortably small size of the potty, it's childish aesthetic, and its existence in plain sight for everyone to watch will all contribute to your submissive now burning with humiliation every time they need to 'go.' And this connection between being infantilized and humiliated by their bathroom habits will all only reinforce and contribute to their inevitable return to diapers.

6

FROM PULL-UPS TO PAMPERS

The next big step in your submissive's regression will likely be the transition from night-time diapers, if you've gone that route, to actual diapers.

This is usually a fairly easy thing to do. Simply wait until the submissive's night time diaper has leaked (which they are prone to do, given their typically light padding.)

Your submissive will hardly be able to argue with you when you explain that they need to start wearing 'real' diapers at night because their pull-ups aren't doing a sufficient job 'holding all their weewee.' The evidence of a wet bed will speak for itself.

Or, you can simply explain that real diapers are cheaper, or on discount, and you're not going to put up with their pride costing you more money then you need to spend to take care of their little problem.

Or, you can simply explain how much easier it is for you as their caretaker to change them and clean them up when they're in real diapers, instead of GoodNites, due to the tabs on diapers being more accessible and made for that purpose.

And of course, once you buy real diapers for their night wetting problem, you'll insist that you must change them into their diapers at night, powder, wipes and all, for the obvious reason that they're far more difficult to properly change into than diaper than you can simply pull up like underwear, and you're concerned about their safety.

Once you've gotten your submissive to accept the routine of letting you change them into and out of real diapers, it's fairly easy to manufacture the scenario required to necessitate day time use.

If you've got them on a 'toilet training' regimen, simply don't change them out of their diapers in the morning, (you might explain that you're too busy with work and they need to wait), and wait for them to choose to use their diaper rather than continue to hold their morning pee.

Then, when you return to your submissive, you can feign outrage that they have now lost control of their bladder while they were awake. Expressing disappointment, you can then make the demand that, just to be safe, they must now wear diapers at all times, 24/7, given that they seem to be losing control during the day now as well.

At this point, you might continue letting them use the toilet while they wear diapers (within a strict schedule and under your watchful eye, of course), but it won't be difficult to create the circumstances for another 'day time accident'.

I remember one time, I had put my submissive in the back seat of my car for a day trip. It was a long drive, and I denied him a chance to use the bathroom when he woke up earlier that morning.

He started whining about needing to use the bathroom about half way through the drive, and near the end he was pleading for me to stop. Although I did in fact make it to our destination soon thereafter,

I chose to keep circling the neighborhood until I saw the expression that told me my little boy in the back seat had lost control and wet his diaper.

I couldn't help but smile as I got out of my mini-van, walked to the back seat, and inspected his diaper in feigned horror that he couldn't hold it like a 'big boy,' anymore.

And as you can imagine, I never let him wear big boy pants again after that day.

7

IF ALL ELSE FAILS

BLACKMAIL AND OTHER LAST RESORTS

Should you not find a successful foothold controlling your target submissive's bathroom habits from the techniques listed above, there are still some tried and true techniques if needed.

The first thing to keep in mind is that you should always be thinking about how to negotiate and think creatively about how to convince your submissive to move one step at a time in the direction you want them to go.

For example, I once bet a submissive money that if he let me change him into a night diaper, he wouldn't be able to keep it dry.

Any tricks I might have pulled to 'help' him wet were out of the question, as now he was determined to keep his room locked out of wariness for any 'tricks' I might pull.

But even though he didn't wet his diaper that first night, it was worth paying him the $20 in the morning just so that I could have him cross the psychological threshold of letting me change him into a diaper. Once he took that first step, it was so much easier to manipulate him into wearing diapers 24/7 using all the other tricks in my bag.

The next option is a sort of blunt force option. I have a friend who was a landlady to an 18-year-old boy she wished to regress. When the boy refused to wear night protection or obey her potty training rules, she resorted to an ultimatum — that he either start wearing diapers full time (to prevent her furniture from being ruined by his accidents), or that he find another place to live.

Because she rented to the boy at rates far below market value, it wasn't hard for the boy to agree to wear them 'temporarily,' until he found another place with a landlord who 'wasn't a psycho.'

Then, when the boy was finally diapered, the landlady transitioned to the final technique of last resort — blackmail.

She took photos of the boy wearing his diapers and getting his wet diapers changed (she even had video of him masturbating in his diapers!) She threatened to release the photos and videos to all his family and friends if he didn't obey her from now on.

The beautiful irony of this blackmail technique is that every day the submissive continues living as a baby for the domme, the domme is able to continue to build her blackmail folder with all the pictures and videos of the submissive in his compromising position.

From what I last heard, that boy is still living with his land lady as her full time, diapered baby. And when I last talked to them, they both seemed as though they'd never been happier.

The moral of this story is that there are many ways to skin a cat. Or in this case, to regress a boy back into diapers.

PART II
BACK TO BABYHOOD

This next section will be discussing the basics of your submissive's new, adult-babied life.

The final catalyst for your little's transformation from accident-haver to full time baby could be as simple as a dramatic 'final straw,' you pick out of any number of behaviors.

Perhaps your submissive starts to argue and disobey your rules. Perhaps they take their diaper off in protest, and make a mess in their bed sheets as a result. Or perhaps you simply inform your submissive that since you now need to change their diapers every day like their Mommy, they had better start following all of your rules like you actually are their Mommy.

The point is to draw a line in the sand, and declare what amounts to, "If you're going to act like a baby, I'm going to treat you like a baby."

Other variations I've heard include statements like, "I apparently didn't do a good job raising you, so we're going to start over. I'm going to treat you like you're two again until I decide you're ready to try being a grown up."

That being said, I've also had success with never making an official pronouncement to my submissive, and instead just continuing to regress them in all the other ways I sought to once they were diapered full time.

Personally, I have a theory that once a submissive starts wearing diapers full time, and they depend on their caretaker for their diaper changes, a deep psychological transformation takes place within them. They become inherently more passive and accepting of their freedom being stripped away and replaced with the features of a life of a baby.

Either way, like in the early phases of diaper regression, it may be helpful to at times be incremental and patient as you implement the necessary changes and rules that will determine your adult baby's new life. (For example, I enjoy buying diapers that are gradually thicker and thicker over a period of weeks.)

Other times, it may be to your advantage to be swift. (Like replacing all of the furniture in their room with their 'new nursery' while they are out of the house.)

A couple things to keep in mind going forward are:

1. **You must achieve clarity on your little's new age.**

You should identify, for yourself, the age you want your little to be regressed to, and be consistent with that goal. By mentally picturing your submissive as now living as say, a two-year-old, it will give you a target and constancy in terms of how you treat them overall.

2. **Be Firm.**

Some domme's may be nervous as they implement these more all-encompassing changes, especially on a first time submissive. It's important that you NEVER BACKTRACK or let the submissive return to their adult status, at least if you can help it. Know that if you give your little an inch (say by letting them take their diaper off for a day), they'll take a mile (and try to stop wearing diapers altogether), and it will be that much harder to regain control over them again.

3. This is Permanent.

Always keep in mind that this shift is permanent as long as you're in your little's life. The more you internalize this and reflect it in your actions and behavior around the submissive, the easier it will be for them to make this transition.

Happy Dominating!

8
THE POWER OF A PAIR OF SCISSORS

One of my favorite things to do when I'm reverting a submissive back to diapers full time is use a pair of scissors to cut up their old underwear in front of them while they watch.

Of course, alternatively, some domme's enjoy it when their submissive returns home one day, opens their underwear drawer, and sees that their underwear is now all gone, replaced by a drawer full of disposable diapers.

But for me personally, I enjoy waiting for the proper catalyst (say, a day-time accident on behalf of the submissive), dragging the submissive into their bedroom, and forcing them to sit in their wet pants as I use a pair of scissors to cut up their 'big boy' underwear one by one.

The psychological impact of seeing their previous underwear destroyed before their eyes, making crystal clear that the only 'underwear' they'll be wearing from now on is diapers, is exquisite.

This same technique can also be used for their 'adult clothes' or even their 'boy clothes' when making those transitions as well. (See those chapters below).

Sometimes a submissive will burst into tears as I perform this act of punishment and transformation in front of them. Don't worry. Just remember, babies are supposed to cry. It's nothing a warm bottle and a diaper change can't fix.

9
PICKING NEW NAMES

Names are a central part of our identity. They are how we both understand ourselves and the world around us.

That's why I think it's important that as the dominant, you pick a new name for your Little as soon as possible.

It could simply be a variation of the submissive's original name (Timothy becomes Baby Timmy or Sarah becomes Little Sarah).

Or it could be a totally new name. It could also be as simple as, 'Princess,' 'Little Baby,' 'Small One,' or even just 'Little.'

If you're implementing sissification into your diaper domination (see that chapter below), you'll want to choose a name that suits their new, girly, sissy status.

Further, just as you assign a new name for your submissive, you should decide the title that you're submissive will now call you. Some examples of titles I recommend for Diaper Dominating domme's are:

- Mommy, Mummy, Mum, Mamma, Mammy or even just Mother

- Grandma, Nana, Granny
- Auntie
- Nanny
- Miss
- Mistress
- Teacher

Other less common but perfectly acceptable domme titles include:

- Countess
- Lady
- Princess
- Queen

The important thing is that once you pick your new title, you must demand your submissive include your new title in their every interaction with you.

Your new name will quickly become, in the mind of your submissive, larger than life, and will attain a goddess-like level of control over them in their mind's eye.

Trust me, it's quite invigorating.

10

BUYING DIAPERS

So, what kind of diapers should you buy??

First thing's first — You will not be buying 'Depends' or any store bought 'adult brief'. Not only are they highly inadequate in their capacity for holding your submissive's mess (they're made for the slightly incontinent, not full time adult babies), they're downright disappointing in appearance and don't even include the proper tabs to put your submissive into their diapers.

We live in a new and glorious era, where the internet and awareness of adult babies has made purchasing real diapers capable of handling your submissive's mess available and plentiful online.

Personally, I recommend the following brands: Rearz and Bambino. They are both highly absorbent, come in large sizes, and have adorable designs to boot!

I also recommend you start storing these diapers in your submissive's bedroom as soon as possible, so that your submissive is always reminded of their diapered state.

What design should you buy?

Well that, my friend, it up to you! And it's the great joy of being a Diaper domme is getting to decide how your submissive looks. Personally, I love the plain white diapers, as they're the most babyish, but I can totally understand the appeal of dressing up your submissive in adorable pink diapers or ones with cartoon prints.

What about Cloth Diapers?

Cloth diapers are also an excellent choice! They offer far more bulk than traditional disposable diapers, helping you to achieve that telltale 'waddle' in your Little's step that is oh so cute. And the addition of large diaper pins is an aesthetic many domme's enjoy.

Don't want to wash cloth diapers?

Then make them a chore for your submissive. Many domme's I know love the sight of watching their submissive clean all their dirty diapers from the week. Then, as an extra level of humiliation, they require their submissive to hang their cloth diapers on a clothes line in the back yard to dry so that the whole neighborhood knows their diapered status.

Plastic Pants?

This is typically a must for cloth diapers. For disposable diapers, these can be a fun or humiliating addition to a submissive's outfit, adding bulk and noise to the submissive's crotch.

For example, if you put your Little out in the yard to play in just their diaper, they will likely ask you to put pants on them. Imagine their surprise when you agree, but then the 'pants' you put on them are clear, plastic and pink!

Further, if you wish for you submissive to make a very big mess and to keep them in it for a long time, plastic pants can keep their mess from spilling to the furniture and elsewhere.

However, personally, I typically prefer to keep my submissive's in just a disposable diaper. For most submissive's, I think this looks and feels like the most babyish option. Especially when their white disposable diaper turns yellow and brown from their daily mess!

Stuffers?

For stuffers, rather than buying the stuffers offered by the brands listed above, I highly recommend buying actual baby diapers. Not only do stacks of baby diapers add a nice aesthetic to your submissive's nursery, but they have an adorable smell that Adult Diapers just don't seem to be able to replicate on their own. More importantly, as stuffers, baby diapers are extremely absorbent and affordable for what they are.

Further, my current submissive has a rather large penis (although I don't let him know that) that tends to point up and stick over the top of his diaper when he's not in chastity, which leads to wet accidents, as you can imagine.

The way I've solved this problem is by using a baby diaper. I can wrap the baby diaper over the top of his penis, then wrap him in his normal adult diaper during a diaper change.

This not only effectively prevents leaking, but I often enjoy taking the soaking 'stuffer' out of the front of his diaper after he's relieved himself, and dropping it in the back seat of his diaper as I then wrap his penis is a new 'stuffer' baby diaper. He makes the cutest faces when he feels the squishy mess on his bottom.

11

DIAPER CHECKS

As a caretaker for your newly, diaper dependent Little, it's crucial that you embrace the habit of checking their diaper as often as possible.

Firstly, I highly encourage you to restrict your Little from ever asking for a diaper change. The psychological sensation of waiting in a wet or messy diaper, and knowing that they have to wait until you decide to check them, is a critical tool of effective diaper domination.

Secondly, there is often nothing more humiliating to a diapered little than the constant reminder of their diapered status by the act of their caretaker constantly sticking their fingers into their diaper to both feel its wetness and look down into their bottom.

The humiliating act of being 'inspected' like this is critical for reinforcing the submissive's permanently diapered state and reminding them that they have relinquished even the most basic expectation of privacy.

Here are the basic steps of how to perform a diaper check:

1. Approach your Little and wrap your arms around them in a gentle hug.
2. Announce to them (loud enough for any bystanders to hear), "Okay, little one, let's check your diaper!"
3. Reach around the front of your Little and pat and squeeze the front of their diaper. Don't be alarmed when they squirm from you patting their genitals. Try to feel for a more 'lumpy' diaper, which is an indication of wetness.
4. Stick a finger into the leg of their diaper, right near the base of their genitals, and feel for any wetness.
5. Then, to be sure, pull the waistband of the front of their diaper outward. Peek down into the front of their diaper and try to discern any yellow discoloration.
6. Reach your hand down the front of their diaper, all the way to the base of their genitals, and detect whether or not the diaper is wet on the back of their hand.
7. Now that you've assessed the wetness of your Little's diaper, turn them around while they're standing in place, and pull the waistband of the back of their diaper outward.
8. Look down into your submissive's bottom for any brown stains or mess.
9. And then to finish up, make sure to bend down and take a whiff of their diaper to use your sense of smell to confirm what you may or may not have seen.

When you're all done, whether or not their diaper is dry or messy, make sure you give your little a firm pat on the bottom and a kiss on their forehead, and say, "Good job! Mommy's all done checking your diaper!"

And of course, if their diaper is wet or messy, whether you want to change them now or make them sit in their diaper until a more convenient time for you arrives is totally your call!

12

EMBRACING MESSY DIAPERS

Some dommes I know are reluctant to force their submissive to soil their diaper with a bowel movement, citing their own distaste for the idea of cleaning up their submissive's mess.

I think this is a prudish mistake, and I think these domme's are missing out on one of the greatest joys of being a proper diaper regression Dominant.

Forcing your submissive to soil themselves, and then depend on you as their caretaker for their diaper change, is one of the greatest joys a caretaker can have over their submissive. Just think about how transformative it will be for your Little when they realize they no longer are allowed to do the simple act of even cleaning up their own mess.

If you find their soiled diaper to be unpleasant to smell, and their poopy bottom unpleasant to clean, I urge you recognize the power inherent in those feelings.

That is, if you're uncomfortable being near a poopy diaper, imagine how humiliating it is for your submissive to *wear* a poopy diaper in front of you! If you're uncomfortable cleaning their poopy bottom, (by the way, just wear latex gloves, silly!) imagine how humiliating it will be for your submissive to know that the *only* way for them to get out of their mess is to be sat up on a diaper changing table, and have the person they respect more than anyone else in the world lay and hold them down, look at their mess, and clean up their bottom wipe by wipe.

Once you embrace the power inherent in this caregiving act, any feeling of being grossed out before will now be replaced with an overwhelming sensation of power and domination over your submissive, and you'll soon look forward to their poopy diapers every day.

If you need more convincing, here is an entry I wrote in my personal journal one day right after I watched my submissive make a poopy diaper for me to change. Enjoy!

> "There's nothing more thrilling to a nanny than watching her little make a poopy diaper. Personally, I love to watch my Littles squat down and push a load out into their diapers.
>
> It starts when I notice my little begin to withdraw into the corner. My littles know that when they're with me, they're not allowed to leave the room that we're in.
>
> They also know that they must use their diapers for all of their bodily functions (especially poopies!) and when they get that special feeling in their tummy, they usually know what's coming.
>
> My little will start to withdraw from talking or playing, and usually stand in the corner like they're focusing on something. I'll start to silently watch them, anticipating what's to come.
>
> Usually their face will get red, their knees will bend a little, and they might even bite their lip. Sometimes I'll even hear them grunting.
>
> Because my littles are not allowed to wear anything but a diaper in my house, I'll watch for the telltale inflation in the back of their diaper as they drop their steamy poopy into the back of their diapers.

This is usually followed by another grunt and bending their knees even more as they push out their remaining poopy.

Then we'll both hear the telltale 'hiss' of their bladder emptying into their stinky diaper. This part will usually happen two or three times as my little finishes making a messy in their diapers.

Even though it can be harder to push a poopy load out into a diaper than a toilet (especially if the diaper is already full!), I think the effort makes going poopy in their diaper a much more satisfying aspect and lasting part of their overall regression.

After I sense a little has made a poopy in their diaper (as all littles should be doing on a daily basis!) I will pretend not to notice at first.

I'll walk over to the corner (where the little is usually hiding, still squatting in shame) and say, "What's wrong my little baby?"

Usually their face will get red and they'll avoid answering out of embarrassment.

I'll sniff the air dramatically and say, "uh oh, it smells like somebody made a stinky," causing my little to get even more embarrassed.

I'll bend down and sniff the air next to their bottom. "Pee ew!" I'll say out loud.

Then I'll grasp their poopy diaper with my hand and give their poppy diaper a good squeeze and pat. I love smushing a Little's warm, poopy diaper against their bottom.

I'll then pull the waistband of their diaper back and look down at their poopy mess.

"Uh oh! It looks like somebody made a big poopy mess in their diaper!" I'll say in a sweet voice to my little. Usually my little will be very red in the face about this fact.

I'll then check the front of their diaper and stick my fingers near their peepees and say, "My my, you soaked your diaper as well little!"

I'll then place my hand in their bottom again and massage the stinky mess in their diaper as I say it all again.

"Yes, you certainly are one stinky baby in one stinky diaper."

At this point the little will look up at me with their sweet eyes and say, "Nanny, will you change me now?"

Of course, my littles are forbidden to ask for a diaper change under any circumstances. I'll remind them of this, saying "Uh oh little, you know babies don't get to ask for a diaper change. Maybe you need to spend some time in your stinky diapees to learn to behave yourself with Nanny."

I'll then take my little by the hand, walk them back to their play place, and sit them down on to their bottom.

Usually their eyes will widen as they feel their stinky mess squish around on their bottom. I'll then tell them to play like a good little baby while I make them wait for their diaper change."

As you can see, I love making my littles experience their poopy diapers to the fullest. And if you don't yet, I hope you will too someday soon!

13

HOW TO CHANGE A SUBMISSIVE'S DIAPER

For those domme's that have never changed a diaper before, or need a refresher course, here are the basic steps.

Preparation

If you don't yet have a proper diaper changing table for your submissive, you can lay a warm blanket or towel on the floor or bed. However, I recommend at least buying an adorable diaper changing along with the first diapers you buy. It's important that your Little now has a 'space' to understand where they will be changed by you.

Grab your supplies if they're not already handy, including a dry diaper, latex gloves, plenty of baby wipes, diaper rash cream, lotion, and baby powder. Other supplies you might need include a rectal thermometer (for checking to make sure they're not sick) or suppositories (which will be covered in more detail in a later chapter).

Safety Note: If you change your submissive on an elevated surface such as a changing table or bed, be sure to keep one hand on your Little at all times. Littles at any age can squirm off the table when you least expect it. Other options for keeping your Little secure will be covered in a later chapter.

Steps:

1. Open up a new clean diaper and place the back half (the half with tabs on either side) under your Little. The top of the back half should come up to your Little's waist. Now the clean diaper is ready to go – and it's there to protect your changing table from getting dirty. (If your Little's dirty diaper is a big mess, you might want to lay a cloth, towel, or disposable pad under your Little instead of the clean diaper while you clean them up first.)
2. Unfasten the tabs on the dirty diaper. To prevent them from sticking to your Little, fold them over.
3. Pull down the front half of the Little's soiled diaper. It's important you take careful stock of the state of the Little's dirty diaper — how wet is it compared to usual? Or how big of a mess did they leave for you?
4. Let the Little know the state of their diaper by making a comment like, "Oh wow Little One, what a mess you made in your diaper for Mommy to clean up!"
5. If your Little has a penis, you might want to cover it up with a clean cloth or another diaper so they don't pee on you while you change them!
6. If your little made a poopy diaper, use the front half of their dirty diaper to wipe the bulk of it off your Little's bottom as you fold it down.
7. Fold the dirty diaper in half under your Little, clean side up. (This provides a layer of protection between the clean diaper and your Little's unclean bottom.) To do this, you'll need to lift your Little's bottom off the table by grasping both ankles with one hand and gently lifting upward. I highly recommend that you always lift your little's legs high up in the air during their diaper changes, just like you would a baby, as it does wonders to communicate their infantile and diapered state to them.
8. Begin gently wiping and cleaning your Little's bottom with

your baby wipes. If your Little has a vagina, wipe from front to back (toward their bottom). This helps keep bacteria from causing an infection.

9. Be sure to clean in the creases of your Little's thighs and buttocks, too. I recommend wrapping a digit in a baby wipes and inserting it into their anus, just to make sure they're 'extra clean'. More on this act will be covered in a later chapter.
10. Make sure to tell your Little what you're doing as you're doing it. For example, "Time for Mummy to wipe up all this yucky peepee so you don't get a rash!" These are important moments for your Little to feel the vulnerability of your control over them.
11. Let your Little's skin air dry for a few moments or pat it dry with a clean cloth. To help treat or prevent diaper rash, you may want to apply rash cream or petroleum jelly. (The best defense against diaper rash is a dry bottom, achieved through regular diaper checks and changes.)
12. Remove the dirty diaper and set it aside. If you followed step one, the clean one should be underneath your baby, ready to go.
13. Pull the front half of the clean diaper up to your Little's tummy. For a Little with a penis, be sure to point the penis down so they're less likely to pee over the top of the diaper, or use a baby diaper stuffer (described above.)
14. Fasten the diaper at both sides with the tabs. The diaper should be snug but not so tight that it pinches. Make sure the tabs aren't sticking to your Little's skin.

All changed! If your Little has been a good baby during their diaper change, you might want to reward them with a kiss on the forehead or even a gold star sticker on their 'good baby' chart!

14
PUBIC HAIR

You absolutely MUST shave your submissive's pubic hair.

While I understand it can sometimes be a pain to do so, just think about how cute your little will look with their hairless genitals.

More importantly, wet and messy diaper changes are far more difficult if you have a mess of yucky pubes to contend with every diaper change.

Need help making it fun? Just keep in mind how humiliating it is for your submissive to have their pubes shaved every week. Their pubic hair is a symbol of their adulthood, and you'll be shaving it away whether they want you to or not.

And when you first do it, you can explain in detail about how they're not mature enough for pubic hair because they poop and pee in diapers, and it's not sanitary to have hair down there when that's the case. I'm sure you'll enjoy the color their cheeks turn.

15

BABY WARDROBE

Once your Little has been changed into diapers, I highly recommend you completely update their wardrobe, destroying or giving away all of their old clothes, and buying entirely new clothes.

First thing's first, a diaper is often an adequate outfit in of itself. I will often institute a rule in my house that the Little is not allowed to cover their diaper with any pants while we're home so that I can always easily assess their diaper by its color from a distance.

Of course, when you go out in public, you may need your Little to wear clothing that will attract less attention to their submissive status, but still make it clear they're wearing a diaper.

I highly recommend you buy shirts for you Little that are both babyish and adorable, and very short, so that they ride up and reveal the top of your Little's diaper sticking out of their pants to any passersby.

For the rest of their wardrobe decisions, I recommend you buy clothing that is babyish or infantile in nature, such as a Barney T-shirt or loose fitting pants.

When you're at home, you'll of course have far more freedom to dress your Little in whatever suits you, so I encourage you to have fun and buy whatever you think will look the cutest!

Some example wardrobe items you can buy for your Little are:

1. Onesies
2. Sleepers
3. Rompers
4. Dresses
5. Bonnets
6. Bibs

The key thing is that your Little knows that you will decide what they wear from now on, all day, every day.

16

THE NEW NURSERY

When you're ready, I recommend taking the step to swiftly transform your Little's bedroom into their new nursery.

The way I like to do this is to set up a playdate for the Little somewhere else. Then, while they're out of the house, I immediately get rid of all of their old belongings, and replace it with what they'll need for their new nursery.

Here are the basics:

The Diaper Changing Table

The Little's new change table is a pillar of their new diapered state, a daily reminder of where they lay down to be totally controlled by their dominant every day.

I recommend stacking it with all the supplies you'll need, including fresh diapers, baby wipes, baby powder, diaper ointment, gloves and suppositories — not just for your convenience — but so that the

Little is always visually reminded of the supplies their nanny needs to take care of them.

Their Crib

Sleeping in a proper crib, with rails that prevent them from getting out and getting into trouble, is crucial for your Little's psychological development.

Some ABDL sites sell cribs or the rails you need to accomplish this task. But it's always possible to be creative and make your own as well! The important thing is that it looks and feels like a crib for a baby.

Baby Wardrobe

Like I discussed above, you should immediately remove all of their old adult clothes, and full their closet up completely with all the onesies, jamies, overalls, and short cut t-shirts that will define their new wardrobe.

Of course, there will still be times when your little needs to put on adult clothes over their diaper for specific public outings. I recommend you keep these specific clothes in your own room so that they know only you can provide that clothing when you decide it's appropriate.

Diapers

And of course, you should pile stacks of their diapers as high as possible so that your Little can always see with their own eyes that you'll never run out of diapers to change them into.

Wallpaper

Don't forget to include an adorable wallpaper print — either classic floral or pink and blue!

The Magic of Smell

Lastly, smell is one of the most enduring sense memories we have, and the babyish smells you surround your Little with will do wonders to regress them back to their long-forgotten toddlerhood.

Here are some extra ways you can enhance and use the power of scent to regress your submissive:

- Baby Powder. Heap on as much as possible whenever possible. Not only will this protect your submissive from a rash, but the smell tends to stick and float about, turning their nursery into a babyish smelling haven.
- Buy and use actual baby diapers. As referenced above, I recommend you use them as stuffers in your Little's adult diaper. One of the reasons is that in addition to being great stuffers, baby diapers have an undeniably babyish fragrance to them that adult diapers are yet to replicate. I recommend even holding a fresh baby diaper up to your submissive's nose during diaper changes to give them a whiff of the pleasant and transformative scent. Fun!
- I highly encourage you to dispose of your submissive's wet and messy diaper into a loosely covered diapered pail next to where they will be sleeping. The odor of their soiled diapers will begin to accumulate over time, and soon they will be unable to escape from the undeniable, distinct, infantile and humiliating scent of soiled diapers in their room. They will then begin to identify and even cherish the smell, regressing them further into their own helpless toddlerhood.

17

FEEDING

Feeding your Little is second only to diaper changes as the most important method of bonding between you two. Depending on what age you decide your Little to be, their diet will consist of some ratio of solid foods, baby food, and milk (milk will be covered in more detail below.)

First thing's first — you must acquire a high chair to feed your Little in. You can acquire an adult high chair on various ABDL or medical websites, or you can make one yourself.

I highly recommend you develop a feature in the high chair that both locks your Little in their seat (for example, a chest harness or strap that secures them to chair) and wrist restraints that keep your Little from using their hands (I like to place these below the tray I'm feeding them on.)

By establishing the routine of always locking your Little into their high chair for every meal, whether it's solid food or baby-mush, you'll take great strides in making them totally dependent on you for one of their most basic needs — eating.

Make sure you put a bib on them, as Little's are always messy when they eat! If you're feeding them solids, make sure to cut their food into very small pieces.

Feed them bite by bite, and make sure to tell them what a good Little they are for every bite they take. Expect that they will spill, slobber and drool, of course, as the feeding goes along.

If you're feeding your Little baby food, I recommend getting a spoon that is slightly over-sized, and feed them too quick for them to breathe between bites. This will result in baby food spilling down their cheeks and chin, and in them gagging and spitting up, making them feel like a real baby when you feed them.

Is your Little reluctant to eat the food you provide?

Well then, you can rely on a classic 'mommy' trick as old as time. Simply pinch their nose and wait for them to open up to breathe. And when they do, just keep shoveling their food in.

One of my domme friends has a pinching plastic nose plug for just this occasion. She now puts it on her Little every time she feeds them in the high chair. She says they never refuse her spoonfuls of food anymore. Not for very long anyway!

As for baby food (which I think is much more fun to feed your little than big kid food), actual jars of baby food are too small in quantity and not nutritionally sustainable in the long run. Therefore, I encourage you to make your own!

Simply blend up a mix of all the food your Little needs for a healthy diet into a mushy paste. It will taste terrible of course, making feeding it to your submissive that much more fun to do! With every bite of mush, you know you'll submissive will be getting the nutrients they need, and the constant reminder that they are a total and utter baby under your control!

Milk

Milk is crucial for the nutrition of a Little. That's because warm milk comforts them and makes them feel full, special and sleepy in only the way that warm milk can. It's also important for helping them pee in their diaper as much as possible which also reminds them of their Little status.

Bottle feeding is the most common way domme's feed their Littles, but I have a friend who still lactates. Her lucky Little gets to drink real baby milk! You can find guides online for learning how to induce lactating in yourself if this is something you're interested in.

Even if you aren't actually lactating, one of my favorite ways to reward my Little for being good is to give them a chance to have a suckle at 'Mommy's Milk Jugs,' even if they haven't actually made milk in a long time!

18

TAKING TEMPERATURES

Should you ever suspect your Little to be running a fever, it's crucial that you use a rectal thermometer to get an accurate temperature. Littles are incapable of holding a regular thermometer in their mouth long enough for an accurate reading, and your baby's health is too important to risk that!

Here are the easy steps to taking a rectal temperature:

1. Put petroleum jelly on the bulb end (thin, shiny end) of the thermometer.
2. Lay the Little face down and spread their buttocks apart.
3. Insert the bulb end of the thermometer into their anal canal no more than an inch. Just make sure the shiny metallic part is inside.
4. Keep the Little from struggling as you don't want him to accidentally push the thermometer in too deep.
5. Keep the thermometer in place until the thermometer beeps or at least one minute. (Sometimes, if a Little has been naughty, I'll keep it in a little longer.)
6. Remove the thermometer and read the digital result.

19

TOYS

It's important that you dispose of any 'adult' toys your Little still may have around — like video games, computers, TV's, iPhones, etc. — and replace them with all the age appropriate toys they'll need to stimulate their baby brains and keep them entertained while they play in their diaper in the other room.

Here are suggestions for age appropriate toys:

1. Wooden Blocks
2. Stuffed Animals
3. Costumes for playing 'Dress up'
4. Jigsaw Puzzles (make sure it's appropriate for ages 3 and under!)
5. Crayons and Coloring Books
6. Easy Bake Oven and 'House' Toys
7. Baby legos (NOT big kid legos, which babies can choke on!)
8. Hand puppets (These can be extra fun for a Mommy and her Little to play with together!)
9. And Playdough!

If you do let your Little watch TV without you with them on your lap, I highly recommend you install parental safe controls to make sure they only ever watch programming intended for ages three and under.

Or even better, I removed the buttons on the TV set that's at my house. Now, I turn the TV onto to the pre-school channel and leave the room with the remote, so my little is never tempted to try and change the channel. Who knows what their little minds could accidentally be exposed to on other TV channels nowadays!

20

OTHER ACTIVITIES

Story Time and Books

The best way for you and your Little to bond is story time. Not only is this a great time for you to cuddle and bond, but it's a way for you to teach your Little about the world.

For example, my favorite story book to read to my Littles is called 'The Baby who climbed out of her Crib.' Not only does it have adorable pictures of a baby to remind the Little of who they are, but it drives home an important lesson — they are never to leave that crib!

Nursery Rhymes

Nursery Rhymes are one of the fun ways you can sing to your Little and relax them as fall asleep on your lap or in their crib.

Here are a few nursery rhymes to get you started!

3 Blind Mice

> *3 Blind mice,*
> *3 Blind mice,*
> *See how they run!*
> *See how they run!*
> *They all ran after the farmer's wife,*
> *Who cut off their tails with a carving knife.*
> *Did you ever see such a thing in your life,*
> *As 3 blind mice?*

Baa, Baa, Black Sheep

> *Baa, ba,a black sheep,*
> *Have you any wool?*
> *Yes sir, yes sir,*
> *Three bags full.*
> *One for my master,*
> *And one for my dame,*
> *And one for the little boy*
> *Who lives down the lane.*

Incy Wincy Spider

(Or Itsy Bitsy Spider)

> *Incy wincy spider,*
> *Climbed up the water spout.*
> *Down came the rain,*
> *And washed poor Incy out.*
> *Out came the sunshine,*
> *And dried up all the rain,*
> *And Incy wincy spider,*
> *Climbed up the spout again.*

Naps and Bedtime

Your Little's bedtime should be no later than 8pm (although 7pm is advisable.) I also recommend you put your Little down for a nap at least once a day. Littles need lots of rest!

You can even adjust their bed time as a means of behavior control if needed. More on that in the punishment section later!

Baby Monitor / Nannycam

Make sure to monitor your baby while they're in their bedroom at all times.

You can either use a classic audio only baby monitor, or better yet, a nanny cam.

You never know what trouble your Little could get into if you're not watching! For example, playing with their peepee's inside their diapers! Won't they be surprised when they reach into their diapers, only to have you come running into their room seconds later!

Enjoying Your Sweet Baby

Don't forget to enjoy all the small moments with your Little while you have them!

Cuddling, singing them lullabies as they fall asleep, or even a raspberry on their tummy during a diaper changes are all the ways you can show the Little that you love them and that they're yours.

PART III
RULES FOR LITTLES

When the time comes, you will need to explain to your Little in no uncertain terms all the rules that they will need to follow while under your care.

I've decided to share a long list of rules I've used with my submissives, not because this list is comprehensive or required by any means, but to give you an idea of the rules you can implement.

My advice? Pick the rules that you like, mix and match, and add rules as you go along, and remove them if you're feeling generous. If there's one thing I've learned in my time as a domme, you can never have enough rules (and submissive's can never have enough punishments!)

Sometimes I like to print out the list of rules in really big, rainbow font and put them on my submissive's nursery wall as a constant reminder of what they are and aren't allowed to do. Sometimes I even like to make them put their nose up against that exact list of rules on the wall as punishment when they break one of them.

But I'm getting ahead of myself. For punishments, see the next section below. For now, let's start with the rules.

EXAMPLE RULES LIST

- The Little will use their diaper for all intended purposes. Any request of attempt on behalf of the Little to use a toilet will be punished severely.
- The Little will never ask for a Diaper Change under any circumstance. The Little must always wait to be checked and changed by their caretaker at their caretaker's convenience.
- The Little will never interfere with diaper checks from their caretaker or babysitter.
- The Little will not masturbate.
- The Little will not touch their penis under any circumstance.
- The Little will not reach into their diaper or take off their diaper for any circumstance.
- The Little will never touch their diaper for any reason.
- The Little will always call the Dominant by their full and proper title when addressing them or responding to them. (i.e. Mommy, Nanny, etc.)
- The Little will not talk back or fuss for any reason.
- The little will go to bed at 7pm every evening. No exceptions.
- The Little will not use any 'adult language' and will instead

adopt the vocabulary and manner of speaking of a toddler. Any cursing or swearing will be severely punished.
- When a pacifier is put into the Little's mouth, they will never, under any circumstances, remove it.
- The Little will never attempt to talk while a pacifier is in their mouth.
- The Little will never speak unless spoken to.
- The Little must be supervised at all times. If for any reason the Little is left alone, they must be in a crib, a highchair, a playpen, a harness, or secured in some other way.
- The Little must never leave the room that their caretaker has placed them in without explicit permission.
- The Little must take any directions or follow any rules anyone older than the Little demands while the Little is under their supervision.
- The Little may never consume beverages from any container other than a sippy cup or proper baby bottle.
- The Little may never eat any food that is not given to them by their caretaker while they are in their highchair.
- While in the house, the Little is not permitted to wear pants, shorts, or anything that covers their diaper unless explicitly given permission otherwise.

PART IV

TRADITIONAL DISCIPLINE

This first section of punishments will include 'traditional' discipline and corporal punishment that is still quite common for many parents to actually use in our society.

The impact of the following punishments is more than one might expect on the surface for three reasons:

1. To be punished in *any* way is a humiliating act in-of-itself for a submissive. The nature of these 'disciplinary measures,' and the fact that they are reserved for and meted out only to children in our society, makes receiving them as an 'adult' that much more humiliating.
2. These Punishments are likely to provoke memories of similar actual punishments the submissive received as a child, contributing even further to their psychological regression.
3. The fact that your submissive will be wearing diapers and baby clothes any time they receive any of these punishments

will automatically enhance each punishment's power over your submissive.

For example, a spanking or a time out is, by its nature, embarrassing. But to be spanked on your diapered bottom, or to be sent to time-out only to have to 'make a mess' while you stand in the 'time-out' corner, adds a whole extra layer to these traditional disciplinary measures.

I recommend knowing in advance what punishment you'll enforce for what broken rule so that you have a system that feels internally consistent to you. This will make it less difficult for you to decide what punishment you'll issue when your Little breaks that rule. It will also alleviate any guilt on your part, and make you less susceptible to their whining in protest, as you will already have decided what punishment each infraction deserves.

Sometimes you may wish to inform your submissive about what punishment they can expect if they break a specific rule. Sometimes it's more fun to surprise them.

Finally, it's to your advantage to make the punishment fit the crime. Did your Little one mouth off to you, use big kid words — or even worse — use a curse word? Sounds like you need to 'wash that foul mouth out' with plenty of soap.

Or did your Little climb out of their crib without permission? It sounds like they need to go to be in their crib a few hours earlier at night to help them settle in.

Or did your submissive ask for a change out of their poopy diapers? Well it sounds like an hour of time out sitting in their poopy diaper might teach them about the importance of following rules.

As always, points are awarded if you as the dominant can be creative and have fun with their punishments!

22

TIME-OUT

Time-out is a cornerstone to the modern parent's arsenal of discipline, and that alone makes it a thrilling and humiliating act to subject your Little too.

I like to establish a 'time-out corner' or a 'time-out chair' for my Little to go to. If you use a chair, I recommend you use an adorable, hard plastic toddler chair for them to squat in and think about how naughty they've been. I also encourage you to put a pacifier in your Little's mouth, if it's not already.

As far as length, ten minutes is nice if you need to get your Little to calm down. Thirty minutes is standard for an infraction. I usually don't do longer than thirty minutes unless it's combined with another punishment described below.

Some basic rules of time-out include:

1. The Little may not speak for any reason while in time-out. (This is fun if you're still transitioning your Little to diapers, and you know they're about to have an 'accident.')
2. The Little must not leave time-out for any reason.

3. The Little must think about what they did to end up in time-out and be prepared when they leave time-out to tell their nanny what they learned.
4. If the Little violates any of the above rules, their time-out time doubles.

Also, while in the backseat of my car, I've previously instituted time-out for my little by declaring 'Nose on knees'.

That is, for the duration of our car ride, I've required that the Little bend forward, keeping their 'nose on their knees' for the rest of the ride as a light punishment and a means to keep them from fidgeting in the back seat.

Nose to the Wall

This method can often be thought of as 'an advanced time-out,' because it relies on the same principles. Here's the way I like to do it:

1. Walk the submissive to their 'naughty corner' and have them put their hands behind their back.
2. Pull the submissive's pants down so that their diaper is plainly visible, if it's not already.
3. Grab a kitchen timer with a loud ticker sound. Set the timer behind their back, but don't tell the Little what amount of time you're setting it for. Instead, let them listen to the sound of ticking behind them as a constant reminder of their 'time-out status.'
4. Tell the Little to put their nose in the corner. Tell them that if there nose leaves the wall for any reason, or if they make one peep, that you'll reset the timer behind their back.
5. Leave them there to stand helplessly in the corner in their shame.

Another technique you can add to this is have the submissive hold a penny to the wall with their nose. Tell them that if the penny falls for any reason, you'll reset the timer.

Personally, I love using this punishment if my Little ever asks for a diaper change. How fun it will be when company comes over, and they all get to see the status of my little's poopy diapered bottom as they stand in the corner in their shame!

23

SPANKING

Spanking is the most classic form of domestic discipline, and through the process of regressing your submissive, it will likely be your go-to method of punishment for routine infractions (along with time-out). It behooves you to become well versed in at least the basic techniques I describe for you here.

Padded or Bare Bottom?

The first question you must ask before delivering a spanking is whether the submissive will be wearing their diaper for the spanking or not. (It goes without saying that any pants or other clothing they are wearing will be around their ankles.)

If you have not yet put your submissive back into diapers, then of course you will spank them bare bottom. But if they are wearing diapers, here is a brief list comparing each method.

Bare-Bottom Pros:

- More pain will be administered to the submissive's buttocks through less effort on your part. Further, the pain will be of a 'stinging' nature on the surface of their skin, allowing you

to inflict more pain with less risk of actual or long term injury.
- Depending on the submissive, there may be a greater sense of vulnerability and humiliation to having their naked bottom revealed to their caretaker and any spectators.
- You have access to their bare bottom to prod or even insert a digit into their rectum or vagina, should that suit your desires.

Padded (Diapered) Bottom Pros:

- Having their diapered bottom revealed and spanked, especially to spectators, is a highly embarrassing act for the submissive.
- By not taking their diaper off, you are making it clear to the submissive that even in circumstance where one's undergarments might be removed, their diaper will stay on because their lack of control over their bodily functions is so all encompassing.
- If the submissive's diaper is very wet, or even soiled, having your hand smack their bottom and push their mess against into their bottom and against their genitals can be highly humiliating for the submissive (and highly rewarding for the domme!).

Once you've decided whether or not your submissive will be padded or bare bottom, you should decide the number of spanking they will receive, and let them know this in advance. For a minor infraction, ten spankings is a good baseline. For a more serious infraction, it may be necessary to administer thirty or more spankings.

Here are the basic steps to a classic 'Over The Knee' spanking:

1. Assume the position. Tell your Little to drop their drawers and bend forward over your knee. Instruct them they are not

to get up until you are finished. Tell them that any resistance on their part will only increase the amount of spankings they receive.
2. Warm up. Administer some test spanks and gauge their reaction. Vary the tempo and intersperse spanks with tender rubbing and kneading to warm up both your hand and arm, and their bottom. They will likely shudder in apprehension as they feel you 'preparing.'
3. Begin. Administer your first spank swift and hard to the fleshy region of their buttocks. I like to make my submissive's count their spankings, and if I feel that they've been particularly disrespectful lately, I'll demand that they thank me for each blow. For example, "One! Thank you, Mommy." Any spanks they don't count, I don't count.
4. Continue. Increase the speed of your spanking as you go, methodically ramping up the heat in their bottom.
5. Finish. Try to build to a crescendo and make your final spank the hardest one of all. If you've delivered a successful spanking, you'll often see your submissive in tears at this point. This is a positive sign of their regression and their remorse over making you as their caretaker upset.

At this point, you can either let them finish crying on your lap as you soothingly rub their bottom, or you can pull their pants up immediately and send them over to time-out to sit on their stinging bottom.

A variation to this method that I know some domme's use, is that instead of giving your submissive a fixed quantity of spankings, the dominant will simply start spanking the submissive until whatever amount it takes to reduce the submissive to a sobbing, helpless baby in their lap.

This latter technique can be highly useful to a dominant who feels that their submissive has not yet sufficiently succumbed to the vulnerable emotional state that their caretaker wishes to see them in as a Little.

Finally, while this is the technique of a bare bottom spanking, acquiring spanking paddles, straps, even canes and whips can all become a part of your collection, if that strikes your fancy. Imagine how your Little will quiver when they see the wide range of implements on your wall that you're always waiting to discipline them with.

Happy spanking!

24

WRITING LINES

Does your Little claim to never remember the rules? Well then, I have the perfect solution!

Get out a crayon (the duller the better), and a large piece of paper. Sit the Little down, and tell them they must write down the whole list of rules using their dull crayon.

When your Little is finished, (it will take some time) tell them to do it again with a new piece of paper. And when they're finished with that, have them do it again. Repeat until you're satisfied they've learned their lesson.

The best part? Now you can hang all these lists of rules they wrote in crayon everywhere the Little goes. On their nursery walls, above their diaper change table, even in their crib!

Another variation of writing lines includes having them write down an apology over and over again, explicitly naming their act of misbehavior.

For example, "I'm sorry I was a naughty baby who put his hand in his poopy diaper." How embarrassing! And a fun gift for visitors.

Trust me, once you sit your little down in their poopy diaper to write lines about what they did wrong all night, they'll soon think twice about misbehaving again.

25

BEDROOM DOOR REMOVAL

This technique is more suited for your Little at the earlier stages of their regression, say, before you've already converted their bedroom into a full blow nursery. But I do love it, so I wanted to include it.

Let's say you catch your Little being extra naughty and masturbating (see that full section below), or taking off their diapers, or any number of routine naughty activities they can get up to while unsupervised.

Take that bedroom door away! Not only will they experience a profound psychological loss of privacy (especially if you've done this to their bathroom door as well!), but it will reinforce their feeling that that you are always watching them in a very permanent, visible way.

26

HOLDING THEIR TONGUE

We've all heard the expression 'Hold your tongue'. Well if you're feeling relatively merciful and don't want to ruin a good mood because you and your Little are enjoying time together, you might demand that they 'hold their tongue' should they start to use adult language. Literally.

Have the Little stick their tongue out. Then, have them use their fingers to hold it out. Now, require that they stay like that for as long as you'd like. If they didn't understand how to talk properly like a baby before — they certainly will now as the mumble and drool every time they try to speak!

27

MOUTH SOAPING

Mouth soaping is a very intense technique, despite its innocent enough seeming name. The sensation of gagging on soap is a surprisingly deeply submissive and humiliating act.

Therefore, I urge you to be prudent with this technique. That being said, if your naughty Little just won't learn to stop using naughty words, then you'll just have no choice but to clean their mouth's out!

The steps to a proper mouth soaping:

1. Prepare a clean bar of soap without the Little knowing.
2. Have the Little stand with their hands behind their back.
3. Tell the Little to open their mouth up really wide and close their eyes.
4. Insert the bar of soap into their mouth and tell them to close their mouth on it.
5. They will likely instinctively try to spit it out. Hold the bar of soap in their mouth while you explain that they are to keep it in their mouth until you remove it. Also inform them that if

the soap leaves their mouth, you will reset the length of time for their punishment.

Ten minutes for a first offense is plenty for this method, but if the Little still won't learn, it's perfectly reasonable to double, even triple that time if needed.

This technique also pairs well with other discipline methods. For example, forcing your submissive to keep a bar of soap in their mouth during a spanking is a nice synthesis of both techniques.

28

CHORES

One of the joys of having a new, submissive Little in the house is that you can have them help with the house work! Assigning chores can be both an expectation you have of your Little, or you something you assign them as punishments as needed.

Here is a list of chores to help give you an idea of what you can assign them!

- Scrubbing the toilet
- Organizing the pots and pans
- Scrubbing the inside of small wastebaskets
- Polishing old silver
- Cleaning window wells
- Brushing the animals
- Cleaning the fireplace
- Shaking the kitchen rugs
- Vacuuming the couch
- Moving and vacuuming underneath the furniture
- Weeding the garden (Dressed only in their diaper, of course!)

- Matching up odd socks
- Cleaning the closet, garage, or under the bed
- Ironing
- Alphabetizing the spices in the kitchen

Just to give you an idea of the possibilities!

29

EARLIER BEDTIMES

Your Little's bedtime should already be very early (7pm or 8pm at the latest!), as Little's need plenty of sleep. (And they need the sensation of laying in their cribs in their diapers for long periods of time to remind them of their Little status!)

Bedtime is usually a difficult thing for most Little's to accept, as of course they would like to run around and play with Mommy for as long as possible each day! (Of course, Mommy needs her own time, too! Which she gets when she puts the Little down for their beddie-bye.)

So, an obvious and effective punishment can simply be moving your Little's bedtime up an hour earlier or more for a set duration of time (say, one week).

For one extra naughty Little I once babysitted, they had a bedtime of 5pm for a full month! Their domme didn't tell me what they did to deserve that, but I have my suspicions it involved complaining about bedtime!

When instituting an earlier bedtime, it's important that you not let your Little start getting up or leaving the crib earlier than usual in the morning afterward. Nice try, Littles, it doesn't work like that!

Also, it's important that you not let your Little manipulate you into giving them attention during their long nightly crib time by crying for a diaper change. Make sure to diaper them thick enough to last the duration of their stay in their crib, and don't be afraid to use plastic pants if necessary. (See the section on plastic pants above.)

Your little needs to learn that babies don't decide when they get put in their crib or when they get taken out — that's Nanny's job!

30

DELAYED DIAPER CHANGES

Psychologically speaking, the simple act of wearing a wet diaper or a messy diaper for any duration of time leaves a strong impression on the Little in terms of their helpless status as your baby. Forcing them to stay in those wet and messy diapers, causing them to internalize the sensations they impart to the fullest, is crucial to successful diaper domination.

Therefore, delaying a diaper change can be an effective tool of discipline in of itself. My default punishment for Little's who ask for a diaper changes is simply to extend the length of time they have to wear their dirty diapers for at least one hour.

This simple but effective technique addresses the core of the problem (them not accepting that you determine when they get their diapers changed), by subjecting them to precisely that which they wish to avoid (needing to wait in their dirty diapers.)

This can also be used for Little's who leave their crib at night with the excuse that their poopy bottom was preventing them from sleeping. Sending them back to bed knowing they won't be changed till the afternoon the next day usually sets them straight!

I've also used the technique when my little once got fussy about me changing their wet diaper in a public park near their former 'adult friends'. My solution? I kept them in that diaper for another six hours, then I invited all of his former friends over to watch me change his diaper that night.

Did I mention that by that point, my little didn't just have a wet diaper, but a poopy diaper for them all to see?

Always remember, you're in charge of that diapered bottom! And the only way they're getting out of a messy diaper is when you change them!

31

CRAWLING

Is your rambunctious Little running around the house, acting too loud or obnoxious? Or have they been getting up to no good and snooping where only big kids are allowed — like the kitchen food cabinets?

Then it sounds like you need to institute a crawling rule. A crawling rule states simply that when your Little is in the house, they will never walk or stand on their two feet. Instead, they must crawl on their hands and knees in order to move about.

Not only is this punishment inherently humiliating and babyish, but it transforms your little's world in a major way. After enough time has passed, your Little will soon be used to craning their head to greet guests, or not seeing out the high windows of the house. And of course, their Mommy, who now soars above them in height at all times, will be that much of an impressive figure in their psyche.

32

REDUCING THEIR AGE

Along with crawling, reducing the age of a Little as a punishment can be an effective way to curb their freedom in a way that causes them to internalize the changes as a reflection of 'their' maturity. For example, let's say that your Little currently acts like a diapered three-year-old. You can reduce a year of their age for the next day, letting them gain a greater appreciation of their freedom to walk around as a three-year-old baby, rather than a two-year-old baby.

Here is a brief guideline of 'ages' and their attached behavior for you to tune your Little to.

Age 4

- Capable of communicating with adults by speaking in a childish register.
- Can walk around freely with their caretaker.
- Capable of eating and cutting up their own food.

- Capable of enjoying longer stories and books. They love coloring and playing games.

Age 3

- Can speak in most adult words, but still refers to many things using baby words. (Like Baba for Bottle).
- Capable of waddling most places.
- Can eat solid, children's food, cut up for them by their caretaker.
- The little is very active and playful and will want to start playing with balls, riding scooters, solving puzzles, singing and playing dress up.

Age 2

- Speech is broken and babyish.
- Must alternate between crawling and waddling in 'baby steps.'
- Most of their food is baby mush, but they can have some solids.
- They can play the naming games (pointing at things and naming them), peek-a-boo, playing with clay and squishy stuff, and making silly faces.

Age 1

- Can only babble in the simplest of baby words.
- Can only crawl a tiny distance.
- Can only eat baby mush
- Their fun consists of playing with the simplest of baby toys, peek-a-boo and being read story books.

Age 0 (Newborn)

- Can only giggle and drool. The cannot attempt to speak any words.
- They aren't allowed to even crawl. They can't leave the spot their caretaker put them in.
- They have no dexterity in their hands or fingers.
- They are swaddled and bound, and must depend on their caretaker for every possible need.
- They can only drink milk.
- Their activities are very limited. Playing with basic toys such as rattles and stuffed animals.

As you can see, reducing one's age just one year can provide quite the behavior incentive for a Little!

33
SENT OUTSIDE

Is your Little throwing a temper tantrum? Yelling and screaming and perhaps even throwing things?

Put them outside the house in just their diaper. Let the whole world watch the little diaper girl or diaper boy's show.

I'm sure your Little will still be stomping and crying about their bedtime in their wet diapers when the hot neighbor girl looks out her window to watch.

34
HEADPHONES

Do you have an excessively loud Little? One who screams and yells, can't keep their voice down, or stomps around on the floor?

Teach the value of silence by swaddling them in their crib and putting a pair of fluffy headphones on their head and make them listen to the Barney song turned up on repeat for a couple hours.

I'm sure they'll be more respectful about noise going forward after that.

35

JOURNALING

One of your most powerful tools of regression you have over your Little is the way that you require that they reflect and internalize the humiliating and babyish experiences they go through.

The best way to do this is to have them journal by some means. If they're old enough to write, you can have them write their experiences in their 'special book' in crayon.

If that's not possible, you can have them record a video for their Nana by having them hold up a phone as it records video of them.

After any punishment, have them take ten minutes of time out to reflect.

Then, tell them to journal the experience by answering the following questions:

1. What was the punishment you received?
2. Why did you receive it?
3. How bad were you behaving to have to receive such a punishment?

4. How did it feel while you were being punished?
5. Did it hurt?
6. Were you embarrassed?
7. How embarrassed were you?
8. How do you feel right now?
9. How do your actions and your punishment prove that you are a baby?
10. What are you doing to do different moving forward to not be punished again?
11. Why are you thankful that your caregiver cared enough about you to give you your punishment?
12. What are you going to do for your caregiver to thank her for your punishment?

Of course, you're welcome to add your own ideas to this list. The point is for your Little to reflect, learn and internalize their new, infantile status every time they are punished.

Further, when your Little first starts messing their diapers, I like to have them do a similar journal entry afterward while still wearing their messy diapers, especially if they were holding their mess beforehand. I find that it helps them accept and appreciate that they will be making many messy diapers going forward for the rest of their lives.

36

CASTOR OIL

Castor oil is a cruel, but sometimes very necessary, means of behavior correction. That's because not only does it taste highly unpleasant, but it functions as a powerful laxative for your Little, turning your punishment from a humiliating mouth full of oil to a very humiliating, poopy diaper they must sit in.

In a later section, I will cover more about the importance and use of laxatives while caring for your Little one, but since castor oil is typically used as a punishment specifically, I thought I would cover its administration here.

Here are the steps to administering castor oil:

1. Put the little in their high chair and secure their hands.
2. Remove the large bottle of castor oil from the shelf and pour it into a spoon right in front of them.
3. Grab and pinch their noise, forcing them to open their mouth. (Even if they seem willing to participate, you should still pinch their nose.)
4. Push the spoonful of Castor oil into their mouth and demand that they swallow. Repeat two to three times,

depending on the dose you select for them. Should any castor oil spill down their chin at anytime, I recommend you double their dose.

Castor oil takes time to work through your Little's system, but when it does, they will mess their diaper uncontrollably in a very humiliating fashion. It's not uncommon to see a very red, sweating face, combined with lots of groaning and whimpering, when your little voids their bowels in this way. You've been warned!

Should you wish to enhance the impact of this punishment in the case of severe behavior infractions, I recommend the following:

1. Sit your Little down for their castor oil. Make sure they consume every last drop.
2. Put your Little's nose in the corner for two to three hours. It's likely that they'll make a substantial mess in their diaper during that time. You may also wish to invite guests over to watch them squeal and mess their diaper in the corner.
3. Take your little over your lap and give them a long, hard spanking in their deeply messy diaper. It's likely they'll still be 'relieving' themselves while over your knee while you spank them.
4. Finally, sit them in their messy diaper for a long time out, and have them journal their experience in crayon.

After such a day, I highly doubt they'll be acting up again anytime soon!

37

THE PUNISHMENT WHEEL

Finally, here's a little invention I enjoy that I call the punishment wheel. Pick any of the punishments from above and put them all on a wheel that the Little can spin. Whatever they land on they receive — no ifs, ands or buts!

Why do I love this game? Because the anxiety my little experiences knowing that they could receive any punishment from a simple time-out to a tripe dose of castor oil keeps them always on their toes!

For a gentler version of this game, you can fill the wheel simply with household chores (for chore ideas see that section above).

I think it's very effective for behavior correction, but maybe as a Nanny who take care of Littles every day, I just love a good board game.

38

REWARDS

After reading such a long section on all the punishments needed to keep a Little in line, I'm sure you might be feeling bad for your Little knowing what awaits them when they're naughty.

It's a fair point! Which is why I want to be clear and say that it's equally important to reward you Little when they've started to behave themselves and have stopped putting up resistance to your control over their diapered lives.

Here is a fun sample list of rewards to keep in mind for you Little. It's a great way for a caretaker and a Little to bond (especially after they've just received a punishment for being naughty.)

- Get the Little a Gold Star chart for the kitchen or their nursery, and put happy face and Gold star stickers next to their name on the chart.
- Let the Little pick out the pattern or color for their next diaper! Ooh, the pink butterfly ones are so fun!
- New toys! Such as stuffed animals, coloring books or action figures!

- Extended play time where you read them their favorite book or sink them a song.
- Extended cuddling time where you tell the submissive how special they are to you and pat their head until they fall asleep.
- And finally, you can even come up with a Reward Jar! When the Little pulls a slip of paper from the jar, it includes things like a treat like ice cream, or a trip to the movies, or the chance to stay up five minutes past bedtime.

Just remember, a Mommy punishes her Little when she has to, but she Loves her Little always because she wants to!

PART V

HUMILIATION

Now that we've gotten the basics of disciplining your Little out of the way, I want to spend more time discussing the methods and importance of humiliation to diaper domination.

By now you've probably already gathered the importance of humiliation to your submissive's transformation. After all, a big component of many of the regressing techniques and punishments discussed above include some element of humiliation — some more than others.

That's because what's ultimately separating your submissive from their true, Little self, is the pride they've learned to carry as a shield to exist as an adult in the world.

But since they no longer will exist as an adult, and instead as a Little who will be cared for by you completely, humiliation is a crucial tool to dissolve the wall between the adult they think they are and the baby that they actually are inside.

I encourage you to humiliate your Little as much and as often as possible. It's your greatest tool for transforming their psyche into one that recognizes you as their Dominant and caretaker. You can never humiliate your submissive too much, for if they still find it humiliating to be infantilized and dominated by you, then some part of them is still holding on to the mistaken idea that they aren't your complete and total baby.

Below are several techniques I've found useful to enhancing the humiliation of my diapered submissive. Feel free to use any of them as needed!

USE YOUR WORDS

The most basic act of humiliation you can perform for your Little is to:

1. Always be explaining to your Little what you're doing and why you're doing it.
2. Ask your Little to explain their condition themselves as well.

For example, when approaching your Little and performing a diaper check, make sure you verbally annunciate loudly for your Little and anyone else around the steps involved as you perform each step.

For example, "Let's check that diaper, Little one. Let's check for any peepee down here. Okay, looks good, all dry in the front Little one. No Peepees yet. Now Let's check the back of your diaper for any poopy messes. Wow Little one, no poopy messes back here. Okay, good job!"

Or, during a diaper change, "Okay, time to get your wet diaper changed, little one. Does your wet diaper feel squishy down here on your balls and penis? Let's undo the tabs here and get your soaking diaper off. Wow, Little one, you really soaked your diaper with peepee this time! Lift those legs up! Good boy. Now Momma's gonna wipe all this peepee mess off your bottom so you don't get a rash in your diaper. Good boy!"

By communicating with every step what you're doing and why you're doing it, you will be successfully amplifying the inherently humiliating nature of what you're doing, cementing the psychological impact for your Little.

Further, you should seek to engage your Little's own faculties of explanation when appropriate. (Make sure to require they always address you by your proper title.) For example, when you find your Little with a dirty diaper while you're out with company, you may ask them to explain.

"What happened here, my Little?" You'll ask.

"Nanny, I made a big poopy mess in my diaper," they'll reply in a quiet voice.

"It's quite loud in this restaurant my Little, can you tell me again?"

"I made a big poopy mess in my diaper, Nanny," they'll reply.

"Uh oh. Why did you do that, my Little?"

"Because I'm a messy baby who doesn't know how to use the toilet and so I make stinkies in my diapers," he'll say loudly, for everyone to hear.

These are just the most straightforward examples. I think you'll find that consistently talking to your Little in a sweet voice about their babyish behavior, as well as listening to them do the same in reply, is one of the great joys of being a caretaker for a Little.

40

PUBLIC OUTINGS

Take your little on outings in their diapers!

You can take them out on playdates with you at the park. You can take them shopping with you to the mall. You can take them to the store with you every time you need to buy more diapers for them! (Make sure you always explain to the clerk who the diapers are for and why you're buying them of course!)

Nothing will make your little more babyish than being dragged about by the hand in public spaces, everyone around them pointing and whispering about their diapered condition.

Also, your Little may have gotten used to peeing their diaper in their crib or in your diaper, but it's a whole other level when they have to wet themselves in front of strangers! Let alone walk around with a smelly, poopy diaper they're waiting for Mommy to change!

Next up — Changing that diaper in public!

The idea of being changed in public is a hallmark for most Little's in terms of their anxiety and humiliation about being forced to wear diapers again. So, I suggest you do it as often as possible!

In all seriousness, your Little will need to be changed in public if you don't want them to get a diaper rash. But I also think you'll find a special connection with passersby who get a glance at you changing your stinky little someone.

Here are my favorite places to change my Little's diaper:

- Out in the park on a Sunny day. Simply lay their baby changing mat out on the grass and let the sun shine on their diapered butt as you change them for the whole world to see.
- In any women's bathroom with a baby changing table. I've made great friends with other women this way, who will frequently chat with me about what a 'pretty baby' I have as I change my Little in the crowded restroom. Sometimes they'll even offer to help hold my Little down!
- In the back seat of the car! It's private enough that you won't expect to be bothered, but public enough that your Little will be highly humiliated the whole time.

And don't forget, anywhere you go with your Little, always carry a fully stocked diaper bag with you in case they need a change!

Make sure to disclose to any security who ask to check your bag, "Oh, this is just my diaper bag for this little one. They're about due for a diaper change any moment now!"

41

THROW A PARTY

While I love to take my submissive 'out and about' to subject them to the sensation of strangers all pointing and laughing at their diapered, babyish state, the method I love to use most to subject my Little to public humiliation is to invite people over to our house for a party!

The occasion could be your Little's 'First Birthday', or your own birthday, or any reason at all, really! All you need is houseguests who know about your submissive's diapered status and would enjoy partaking in watching their humiliation.

Possible house guests include fellow dommes (and their submissives), any of your friends, even your family if they might enjoy such a thing! (Imagine your Little's surprise when they get to meet 'Granny'!)

Bonus points if you get the friends your Little had when they were still an 'adult' to come over and admire your Little's transformation. Won't your Little be surprised to see them again!

Here's the way I like to introduce a submissive to their first party:

- Don't tell your Little that you're having a party. Instead, put them in their room to play while all the guests come in.
- Then, when you know that your submissive has likely made a 'stinky diaper' (laxatives may help with timing), go to their room and tell them that you have a special surprise for them in the living room.
- Put a blindfold over your submissive's eyes and pull them out to the middle of the living room. Ask your houseguests in advance to keep quiet.
- Ask your Little to tell you the status of their diaper as you squeeze it. Hold your laughter as they reply, "I made a big poopoo in my diaper, Nanny," in front of all your guests.
- Pull their blindfold off. Have all your houseguests shout 'Surprise!'
- The look on your Little's face as they stand in a stinky diaper in front of such a huge crowd will be priceless.

Here are some more activities and ideas to make your party 'extra special':

- Instead of changing your Little's diaper, have them instead approach each guest at the party and say, "Excuse me, I made a stinky in my diaper. Will you change me?" Enjoy the look on your Little's face as all of your house guests either laugh at them or give them a look of disgust.
- Pass the Little around to each house guest to feel the status of the Little's diaper, either by pulling back their diaper and commenting, squeezing their diapered bottom, or sitting them down on their lap. Pats on your Little's bottom are always encouraged as well.
- Change your Little's diaper on the floor in the middle of the crowd. Have your crowd of friends comment on the status of your Little's diaper.
- Depending on how willing your guests are to participate, have multiple guests participate in the diaper change.

Multiple people can take turns wiping the Little's bottom, or sprinkling baby powder, etc.
- After you change your Little's diaper, have them approach each guest again and say, "I'm sorry I made such a stinky diaper earlier during the party. Mommy says that you can give me a spanking if you would like."
- And of course, if your Little is or was acting up, just because there's guests over is no reason that they'll avoid a punishment! Give them a spanking while all the guests count their spanks. Or stand them in the corner of the party with a soggy diaper!

As you can see, by throwing a party, the sky is the limit when it comes to humiliating your Little back to babyhood!

42

DIAPER DISPOSAL

If diapers come with anything, it's a hefty dose of extra cleaning up. (In addition to the diaper changes themselves!) However, a savvy domme can use this to her advantage as an extra means of humiliation for her submissive.

For example, you can have your Little carry their soiled diapered pale down the street to the dumpster or other disposal site several times a week.

Not only will handling their pile of stinky diapers be a humiliating reminder to them of their babyish status, but anyone who passes by will see the diaper they're wearing and the bin of dirty diapers they're carrying, and they'll immediately know that diaper isn't just for fashion!

Does your Little wear cloth diapers instead of disposables? Even better! Have your Little do all the washing of their cloth diapers, and then have them hang all of them out on a clothing line in the back yard for all the neighbors to see their diapered status.

See, with a diapered submissive, even taking out the trash or doing laundry can become a new occasion for fun!

43

THE POTTY SONG

A recent technique I've implemented with Little's I babysit is that I require they do a 'potty song' and dance before they get a diaper change.

Pick any nursery song that includes some sort of dance steps or moves. This is their new 'potty song and dance' they must do anytime they've been discovered to have gone potty in their diaper. They must do the song and dance in their messy diapers if they want a diaper change.

Here are a couple adorable songs that I've enjoyed having my Little sing (and dance) in front of me:

"Head, Shoulders, Knees And Toes"

Head and shoulders knees and toes
Knees and toes
Head and shoulders knees and toes
Knees and toes
Add eyes and ears

> *And mouth and nose*
> *Head and shoulders knees and toes*
> *Knees and toes*

*For every body part mentioned, the Little points to that part of their body, jumping up and down and wiggling their diaper between stanzas.

"The Wheels on the Bus"

> *The wheels on the bus go round and round,*
> *round and round,*
> *round and round,*
> *the wheels on the bus go round and round*
> *all day long!*
>
> *The children on the bus go up and down...*
> *The doors on the bus go open and shut...*
> *The wipers on the bus go swish swish swish...*

* Every time the Little sings 'round and round', they have to jump up and wiggle their bottom.

That's just to get you started! Of course, you can search for endless number of nursery rhymes with dance moves online. (Teaching a Little a new song and dance is such a great bonding activity!)

I think there's nothing cuter than watching my Little wiggle, wave and squish their messy diaper between their legs as they sing me a little song to remind us both of their adorable and babyish state.

44

STARTING A BLOG

Now that we live in the 21st century, setting up your own blog dynamic blog is easier than ever! Especially now that everybody has a full video production studio in their pocket.

One way to humiliate your submissive is to set up a blog (such as a Tumblr) with them as the star! You can preserve you and your Little's anonymity (if you need to) by cropping their face out of any posts, yet still enjoy telling the world (and showing them) all the details of your Little's new, diapered life.

Don't have the time to maintain such a blog yourself? Make it your Little's responsibility! Impose a rule that your Little must write and submit one post every day about their new, diapered life with you. This pairs well with the 'journaling' method discussed above.

Want to know my favorite content to have my Little produce? Video confessions. Have them explain to the whole world why they're wearing a soaked and smelly diaper. I promise, your Little will have thousands of 'fans' in no time.

I know one domme who, after her Little agreed to become her Little permanently, started a blog featuring all the exploits of their life together. She includes photos and videos of all her Little's feedings, diaper changes, even her Little's punishments.

Not only does the whole world now know all the details of her Little's name, face and diapered status, but they now earn enough commission from monetizing their blog that she has the funds she needs to diaper and care for her Little full time.

Sounds like a fairy tale ending to me!

45

WRITING ON DIAPERS

This is an easy but a fun one, and pairs well with the above-mentioned blog idea (and any other public situation as well!)

Use a big, permanent marker to either write directly on your Little's diaper, their exposed skin, or on a cardboard sigh, that explains to anyone curious who they are and why.

For example:

"Please check my diaper, I don't know how to check myself."

"Do not change this diaper until bedtime."

"Caution: Stinky Baby. Keep a safe distance lest you smell my poopy mess."

The sky's the limit with this one! Let your creativity soar as your put your stinky baby's shame into words directly on them for the whole world to see.

46
THE BIG SHAVE

Everybody knows Little's must have all their pubic hair shaved off, as it's inappropriate, un-baby-like, and only interferes with diaper changes.

But the next step, should you decide your Little needs to take it, is to shave all the hair off their head as well! (Provide they were not bald as an adult already.)

Why, you ask?

Well first of all, everybody knows babies are bald. What more clear way to communicate your Little's babyish status to them than by making them bald in the head as well. And while it may take an extra moment while out in the public for passersby to notice the diaper sticking out over the top of your Little's pants, their stark baldness will be noticed from yards away by everyone around them.

Second, psychologically speaking, most people's hair is a powerful symbol of their autonomy and maturity. Sitting your Little down and shaving their head swiftly and without warning will leave a powerful impact in terms of making it clear which of you decides how old the submissive is.

Third, there's a permanence to shaving your Little's head that inherently lasts longer than say, simply putting your Little in a diaper. Your Little can take their diaper off, put on adult clothes, and run outside, and they might feel like their old, 'adult self' again.

But if you shave their head, it's not likely they'll be able to acquire a wig. Their babyish status will stay with them.

Now of course if your adult baby is now bald, you need to protect that little head from the sun. What better excuse could there now be to put an adorable bonnet on your baby whenever you take them out!

47

PENIS HUMILIATION

To boys (and potentially Trans or other Gender Fluid individuals equipped with them), their penis is a central component of their identity as a masculine or powerful individuals.

You needn't spend more than fifteen minutes eavesdropping on any group of males in their natural habitat before you'll start to hear them referencing their 'dicks', talking about how big they are, or what they're going to do to their counterpart's genitals.

Further, during puberty, many of these men prided themselves on their dicks 'growing hair' and their 'ball dropping'. A common insult I've heard thrown around in such a group is that someone has a 'baby dick.'

Therefore, I think it's crucial that anytime you see your submissive's penis, that you tell them how small it is compared to any penis you've seen before. You might call it a 'baby dick', or cute names like 'their tinkle winkle' or 'itty bitty peepee.'

Because your submissive will likely never touch their penis again (because they're forbidden from putting their hands in their diapers), and you'll be the only one touching their penis, either during diaper checks or diaper changes, you have an enormous amount of power cultivating their perception over the size of their penis (no matter it's actual size.)

I highly recommend that the first time you see your submissive's penis, that you laugh out loud. I promise you that their cheeks will go rosy red as you explain that you didn't think it was possible for penis's to be so small.

As your Little regresses in all the other ways discussed above, by consistently humiliating them about their 'size', the last and most intimate symbol of their masculinity (their penis), will gradually transform into proof of its opposite. Your Little and their 'baby dick' will be a source of great and ongoing humiliation for them (and a source of great pride for you!)

48

HIRING A BABY SITTER

Every domme needs to go out and spend some time away from their Little, perhaps with friends, or even on a sexy date with a 'real man.'

In that case, I highly recommend you hire a babysitter to take of your Little while you're gone!

Make sure your Sitter (most likely a domme herself, but not necessarily), is fully aware of the details of your Little's original age and their diaper regression. (Taking care of adult babies is extra work — don't spring it on someone who isn't fully consenting to the ABDL scenario!)

I highly recommend you hire a sitter who is young and attractive, perhaps even around the age of your Little before they were regressed. This will greatly enhance their humiliation, as they will likely get a 'crush on the babysitter,' as most Littles do in their situation! How embarrassing then when their new crush checks their diaper and finds a big mess to change!

Alternatively, sometimes we domme's just need an extra hand around the house taking care of our Little. Nothing like subjecting your Little to a team diaper change from Momma and the hot new babysitter!

SCHEDULE A DOCTOR'S VISIT

Is your Little not feeling well? Or maybe you think it's just time for an annual checkup?

Taking your Little to the doctor can be a wonderful way to humiliate them in front other authority figured in an intimate way.

I have a friend who is a nurse as well as a domme. She is friends with the doctor where she works, and the doctor is highly supportive of 'diaper regression therapy,' as he calls it, for behavior correction, so he was happy to help play along.

Here's an anecdote of my experience to give you a sense of how you can use a doctor's visit (or a visit to any professional, such as a therapist, a Dentist, or even a tutor) as a fun way to humiliate and regress your Little.

I started by putting my Little in the car without telling them where we were going.

When we arrived and walked into the doctor's office, everyone in the crowded waiting room stared at my Little's visible diaper sticking out the top of his pants in a mixture of fascination, disgust, and curiosity, much to my Little's humiliation.

I remember gleefully describing to the receptionist as I checked him in, "Make sure the doctor knows that he wears diapers and pees and poops his pants. I don't want the doctor to be surprised," much to my shy Little's further humiliation.

When we walked into the patient examination room, I sat my Little down as the nurse came in. (My Little had no idea the nurse was my friend.)

Then the nurse had my Little strip down to just their diaper and sit on the exam table. I then answered a barrage of intimate questions about my Little's 'incontinence' problem in front of my Little as he sucked on his pacifier.

"How often does he pee in his diaper?" She asked.

"I would say about 7 to 8 times a day." I replied.

"Do you think he knows he goes pee in his pants when he goes pee?" she followed up with a serious face.

"I highly doubt it, he seems to wet pretty freely and wait for his Nanny to find his stinky diapers," I answered.

"And is it the same for when he empties his bowels? How intentional is it?" She asked.

"I think it's quite intentional, I can usually see him squatting and grunting in the corner. Then he'll come running up to me right afterward, asking for a 'poopy diaper change," I elaborated as my Little's cheeks burned red hot.

Then, after the nurse was finished, the doctor came in. The doctor submitted the Little to the same barrage of humiliating questions (which I of course answered for him).

The doctor then had the Little lay back, then dramatically sniffed the air. The Doctor looked into my Little's diaper, then called for a nurse.

"Nurse, can you change this patient's diaper? I can't examine him while he's wearing a wet diaper," he shouted loud enough for the whole doctor's office suite to hear. My Little's cheeks went bright red as I feigned apology for my 'stinky boy.'

The nurse came rushing back, and to my Little's surprise, she began to change my Little's diaper on the exam table. I of course offered to help, but the nurse insisted she took care of it because, in her words, "The doctor is picky about making sure diapered patients are thoroughly clean."

When she was finished, the doctor returned and gave my Little a very long examination that involved, among other invasive procedures, squeezing my Little's genitals and sticking his fingers into my Little's rectum while my Little bent over and sucked his pacifier.

At the end of the exam, the doctor turned to me and pronounced his conclusion loudly, "I don't see any obvious problem for his incontinence. I think the best thing to do is just to keep him in diapers at all times, since that seems to be what's working."

"Can do, Doctor!" I replied loudly.

My Little's face went so red with embarrassment and shame, I thought it might have turned that way permanently!

PART VI
RESTRAINTS & BONDAGE

Putting your submissive in a diaper is, in of itself, a form of bondage.

By wrapping them in a cloth and plastic garment that they are forbidden from removing, that they must feel rubbing between their thighs at all times, that they must hear crinkling any time they move, that they must pass their waste into and feel their warm urine or mess press against their skin — every moment they continue to wear a diaper that you put them in, you are pressing them into physical and psychological bondage just as potent as any length of rope or pair of handcuffs.

That being said, as caretakers, there are many times when we must restrain our Little with more advanced tools.

The motivation can vary. Sometimes it's for their safety (we don't want our Little falling out of bed!) Sometimes it's a punishment in of itself (if I catch a Little with their hands in their diapers, they know they'll be locked in their 'special PJs' for the rest of the week). But most typically, it's the means we use to help our Little accept their new, infantile state, by denying them the ability to interfere with their diaper and forcing them to rely on their caretaker for their needs.

Here is a list of tools and methods I've found most useful for my diaper domination work. As always, feel free to mix and match for whatever suits your needs!

50

DIAPER TAPE

Is your Little's diaper always falling off? Then simply use packing tape and wrap it around their waist over and over and over again. They even make plastic tape in adorable colors and patterns you can use for just this purpose.

The best part is when your Little figures out that, with all this tape, they won't be getting their diaper off for long time, until Nanny decides to use the special medical scissors she has to get them out!

51

ADDING BULK

One of the most central ways a diaper makes itself known to the wearer is the added bulk it adds around their crotch, particularly in between their thighs and under their groin!

One way I like to increase your submissive's tell-tale 'diaper waddle' and their overall babyish sensation is to add bulk between their legs.

You can keep adding stuffers — either adult diaper stuffers or actual baby diapers between their legs — or keep wrapping them up in multiple diapers. Even adding towels between their legs is a nice way to increase the sense of padding on their groin.

Just make sure that if you add additional diapers or baby diapers, then you put a few small slits into the bottom of the diaper, allowing urine to leak through the diaper into the diaper below it when it reaches capacity. Otherwise, your Little's urine will simply spill out the legs of their diaper far before when they've reached capacity (and they've gotten to feel all that wet, bulky, heaviness between their legs!)

52

RESTRAINTS ON THE CHANGING TABLE

When you buy a diaper changing table for your little, I highly recommend you install a large waist belt that you can always pull over and secure your Little with, as well as two wrist restraints you can use to secure your Little's hands (always above their heads.).

I encourage you, from the first diaper change with your Little, to always, without exception, use these restraints when they're on the changing table, even if you feel like you don't need them.

Firstly, it makes sure that your Little is safe, and won't be rolling off the table while you change them.

Secondly, it communicates to the Little a strong sensation of vulnerability and dominance to know that while you access and clean their most intimate parts, they'll barely be able to lift their head high enough to watch the process, let alone touch anything below their waist with their hands.

Also, it makes your job as the caretaker easier knowing that when you, for example, start probing their anus with your fingers or inserting suppositories into their bottom, that even if they squirm, they won't interfere with the work you're doing.

I've also installed a mechanism on my diaper change table that is a bar that comes out of the wall above the change table, and allows me to lift my Little's feet and secure them up and open during the diaper change.

Not only does this impart a strong babyish sensation to my Little to be secured at all four points in this way, it helps me have full and unrestricted access to my Little and their bum for every diaper change.

Also, I recommend using restraints that 'click' when you buckle them, as they sound very babyish, and create an audible cue for the Little to know when they're being restrained.

53

SIGHT AND SOUND

A means to blindfolding your Little should always be on hand for a dominant.

This could be a simple piece of baby blue cloth you tie around their head, a pink sleeping mask you drop over their eyes, or a bonnet you tie on backwards.

That's because taking away your Little's sight is a profoundly effective way to calm them down if they're acting up, it helps them focus on and internalize the physical sensations of you babying them, and when they can no longer see, they're automatically more dependent on you for their basic needs.

For example, I find it nice to blindfold my Little for their diaper change because it helps them focus on the smell of their diaper coming undone, the cool sensation of me wiping their genitals, and security of a fresh new diaper being wrapped around their waist.

It's also an easy addition to any other bondage method listed below, should you wish to enhance their feeling of losing control and being utterly dependent on you.

Similar to blindfolding, thick, sound proof ear muffs can be a great tool to also have on hand.

You want to make sure to use ear muffs that are comfortable for long term use as well as adorable (I love the Barney ear muffs I have in my collection.)

Taking away your Little's ability to hear will increase their feeling of dependence, just like when they're blindfolded. It will help to isolate them into their own little world where they can focus on the sensation of using their diaper, rather than the world around them.

For example, imagine having your Little stand in the naughty corner while you have guests over. By putting ear muffs on them, in addition to a blindfold, you take away their crucial ability to even sense if someone else is in the room (say snickering and pointing at their diapered state.)

Or even more simply, when you walk your Little around a party, showing them off to all your guests, it will be a deeply infantilizing feeling for them to not be able to hear or understand what anyone is saying about them. They'll simply see others smiling and laughing at their diapered bottom as their caretaker walks them around.

Or if the submissive is in their crib, by having ear muffs on, they won't even be able to hear the door of their room opening in order to anticipate their morning diaper check. They'll simply be surprised by the invasion of a finger into their diaper out of the blue.

As you can see, ear muffs, like a blind fold, are a very effective means of regressing your Little in a very practical and easy way.

54

KEEPING HANDS OUT AND DIAPERS ON

One of the first obstacles you're likely going to run into as you transition your Little full time into diapers is their habit of either:

1. Reaching into their diapers.
2. Removing their diapers.

Of course, a Little must be strictly forbidden from doing both. A Little might reach into their diaper to play with their genitals, scratch an itch, or heaven forbid, masturbate in their diapers. Needless to say, all of the above is highly unsanitary, and it's a Nanny's duty to prevent that from ever happening under your watch.

A Little is likely to remove their diaper either because they're under the mistaken impression that they don't need one and they don't like being a baby anymore, or by accident, as some Little's are prone to do. This is also highly unsanitary, as it runs the risk of the Little making a mess without their diaper on.

I think the next few tools are the first line of defense against these behaviors, but almost all of the restraints listed below can be of use for these purposes.

RESTRICTIVE MITTENS

Medical, locking mittens that restrict your submissive's use of their fingers are a crucial tool for any domme to have.

This item is relatively cheap and can be bought at any medical supply store. They are essentially bulky mittens that lock around your submissive's wrists, preventing their removal.

They're so large and full of cotton that they prevent your Little from most tasks that require any sort of dexterity, such as turning a door handle. As an added bonus, they simulate pretty closely the capabilities of a toddler, making them that much more appropriate. (For example, your Little will still be able to drink from their milk bottle if they hold it with both hands. How cute!)

These are a useful first line of defense against diaper removal because your submissive's hands will be too wrapped up to be able to effectively undo the tapes around their diaper. Further, they'll be too bulky for your submissive to reach their hand into their diaper. They'll also prevent your submissive from using their fingers to rub their genitals through their diaper in a dexterous way (although they'll still be able to rub their cotton-wrapped fist against the front of their diaper).

These mittens also pair well with all the other types of bondage discussed in this chapter and usually can be added without interference. This is useful in case your little Houdini Little is skillful at wriggling out of their wrist and ankle cuffs and unlocking their crib at night. By taking away the dexterity of their fingers, I doubt that will happen again anytime soon!

I've also seen these sorts of mittens for sale in adorable prints and patterns, if you wish to make them a more permanent part of your Little's wardrobe. Personally, I think it's a great idea. What better to reduce your Little to babyhood than to make sure they can never so much as hold a spoon without your help again!

56

LOCKING PLASTIC PANTS

The next layer to preventing diaper removal or interference is to use a pair of plastic pants with a simple lock on the top. These are now highly available to buy online, and typically feature a small chain around the top and a small luggage lock.

Plastic pants are a useful item to put on your Little in general, as they both add bulk, heat and crinkliness to your Little's diaper (adding to their submissive, humiliated state), while also preventing the mess in their diapers from getting on their clothes or your furniture. Further, the fact that they are transparent makes it easy for you to visually check their diaper from afar, while also subjecting them to the embarrassment of having their diaper remain visible to everyone around them.

When you pull the plastic pants up over your Little's diaper, it can be great fun to subject them to the clinking of the chain, as well as the sound of the lock clicking shut. I recommend you show them the key to the lock in your hands, and say something along the lines of, "Just a reminder little one, Mommy controls the key to those diapers. It's right here, in my control. And you're not going to see it again or get out of those diapers until Mommy says so."

If you plan to keep your Little in a messy diaper for an extended period of time, locking plastic pants are a great tool to use, as they provide the service that plastic pants do of keeping their mess in their pants, they keep your Little from taking their diaper off in desperation, and they add an extra level of psychological impact for your Little when they see and feel the locking mechanism on their pants at all times.

57

LOCKING PAJAMAS

My personal favorite way to keep Littles from getting out of their diapers or sticking their hands where they don't belong is to use locking pajamas, particularly at night.

These are freely available to buy in adult sizes, as they are of tremendous benefit to parents of small children or special needs individuals who take their diapers off at night.

The way these work is that they are typically footy pajamas that have a zipper up the back that either locks or fastens securely at the top. You can have your Little step into their jammies for bedtime, then zip them all the way up and secure the zipper, knowing there's no way for them to even get out of their footy pajamas, let along touch their diapers.

This is my personal favorite because it avoids the chain of the plastic pants, which some domme's find to be disruptive to the adorable baby aesthetic they wish to impose on their submissive, yet does the job of preventing diaper interference just as well, if not better.

The fact that this restraining system seamlessly integrates into an article of clothing you would put your Little in regardless (footy pajamas), is all the better in my opinion. I think this is helpful because it tells the Little that being prevented access to touching their diapers isn't just a special, additional punishment (although sometimes it is that), it's in fact integral to what they sleep in and wear every single day. It's their new normal. The adorable, fleecy comfort that footy pajamas provide merges with the feeling of infantile helplessness in the submissive, making a tremendous and important impact on their total regression and dependence on you as a caregiver.

And did I mention they're adorable?

58

OTHER ARTICLES TO SECURE DIAPERS

Besides plastic pants and footy pajamas, there are two other articles I thought worth mentioning to help inspire you to see the myriad of ways one can keep their Little safely diapered.

The first is a beautiful diaper cover I've seen for sale on Etsy that's made of thick canvass, two simple straps, and either a Segufix Lock or a Magnetic Key to keep your Little's diaper on. I think this diaper cover looks adorable, and might be a better option than traditional plastic pants or locking pajamas when your Little's outfit needs to be more discreet.

The second item is a pair of 'safe shorts' I've seen for sale that are made of kevlar and include a combo lock built into them. They're sold as an item of safety equipment meant to prevent someone's shorts from being removed against their will in the case of a sexual violence.

However, putting your Little in these in a diaper and keeping the combination to the lock to yourself seems like an excellent method of insuring diaper compliance! Especially if you have to let them out of your sight (say, drop them off to go to school.)

The best part of these locking shorts? If your Little tries to yank the waistband or legs open, a pin is pulled from a built in, device which sets off a 140-decibel alarm. Seems like quite the effective way to let whoever is in charge know that your Little is up to no good!

59

CRIB RESTRAINTS

When you build a crib for you Little, I recommend you install crib bars high enough to the ceiling to prevent them from climbing out, or installing a top portion of the crib that you can keep closed to prevent them from leaving in the night and getting up to trouble.

But sometimes you need even further restraints on your Little while they're in their crib. This may be because your pesky Little seems to be able to undo the traditional crib locking mechanism you use, or because in their crib they're up to naughty behavior (such as sticking their hands in or removing their diapers.)

You can buy medical wrist restraints and ankle restraints and tie your Little's limbs to the four corners of the crib fairly easily for a first line of defense.

Need even more security? I recommend investing in a Segufix bed restraints system or a similar brand. The company offers modular restraint options for your Little's needs.

I love locking my Little's head to toe in a full bed restraints when they've been naughty. Not only does it give me the peace of mind knowing they won't be leaving bed or removing their diaper, the whole process of wrapping them up for their restraints is great fun. Every strap I tighten, every nob I turn, every lock I click is a reminder to my Little of how naughty they were, and when I leave them there all night in a wet diaper, they'll usually be very well behaved for many days afterward.

60

LEASHES AND HARNESSES

Child friendly leaches and harnesses are very common nowadays for parents to keep their children from running off while they're out with them.

As dominants, we can use similar leashes for the same reason with our Littles! A harness can also be effective to keep a rascally Little from escaping a play place you've set up for them in your house. You can also wrap a harness up underneath their legs to help prevent attempted diaper removal.

You can even make your own little harness and leash. Simply get any type of adorable harness that will fit them online, lock them into it, and use a puppy leash on their back to keep them close by.

Think about how cute you'll be walking down the path in the park with your little one waddling in front of you, chasing butterflies in their diapers.

Or maybe when you take them to the play place, when you see them making poopies in their diaper, you can give them a little yank from behind, causing them to full down and land on their diaper on the safe gym mat, causing a big squishy mess for them to sit in!

61

ADULT BABY STROLLER

Nothing beats taking your baby for an afternoon stroll with their hands and feet secured in their new, adult baby stroller!

Won't it be fun when you encourage your friends and passersby to stop over and comment how cute they are while they're stuck in their stroller? Especially when they have to go peepee while being tied up and wheeled around?

If you can't afford to buy an adult baby stroller or make one yourself, a normal wheelchair, one made for those with advanced special needs, does the job just as well! Especially when you simply add some hand and feet restraints to the device.

I have a wheelchair that I've had a friend paint bright pink for me, so that when I wheel my Little around, everyone knows that he's my cute, adorable adult baby, and they all comment as such.

And on that note, I highly recommend you keep your Little in a special made car-seat so they're safe when traveling with you at all times.

It's important that you always put them in the back and secure their hands and feet so they're safe when you travel!

62

THE BOUNCY SEAT

You've surely seen the bouncy seat for children that allows them to sit in a secured seat and bounce up and down!

Well with a little home construction effort, or if you're willing to buy a slightly more expensive one for your Little made for adults, you can put your Little in a bouncy seat as well!

Imagine the look on your Little's face as you have them climb into the seat that hangs from above and barely let's their feet touch the ground. Imagine how cute it will be to have them make a peepee in their diaper while they bounce up and down like a real baby, giggling as the warm diaper bounces and presses against their genitals.

Or best of all, imagine putting a naughty little in the bouncer after they've made a stinky diaper. Bouncing up and down in their mushy diaper, feeling it squish against their bottom and groin every landing and take-off.

What fun!

63

STRAIGHTJACKETS

Straightjackets are also a great option within the realm of medical restraints. They have tremendous power to visually and viscerally remind the Little of their dominated status while they wear a straightjacket, partially due to the fact that the straightjacket is such an icon of being medically controlled in our culture.

A straightjacket is also very practical because it gives the Little enough mobility so that they aren't a burden on you caring for them (they can still walk around and you can still check and change their diapers with ease), while still putting them in a highly bonded, claustrophobic head space by virtue of the way it wraps and holds their whole arms and hands tightly around them.

Buying an adorable, well stitched, straightjacket with many shiny buckles to keep in the closet for whenever your Little needs some 'jacket time' is a great investment. Your Little will shudder anytime they hear the clinging of the jacket's rings, leading to a tremendous regression and psychologically dominating effect.

64

PACIFIER GAGS

Your Little will have a relationship with the pacifier you give them, and sometimes that relationship will be contentious. That's because while you know when it's important for your Little to calm down, be quiet, and suck their paci, you'll find that, especially in the beginning, frequent instances of them spitting their pacifier out either out of insolence or laziness.

Therefore, using a simple strap to wrap about their head and keep the pacifier in their mouth is a helpful way to know that they won't be making noise or causing trouble when you need them to be well behaved and quiet.

You can use your own simple strap that you wrap, sew or glue to the pacifier, or you can buy any number of pacifier gags for sale for this purpose.

One more note on pacifiers — I highly suggest you buy a pacifier with the thickest bulb possible.

(There is a pacifier that you can buy at ABDL outlets called the Nuk 5 that is fairly large and affordable. But even better, if you can afford it,

I suggest you buy a pacifier made special by a German company called the MEGA Size 10+. As of now is sold by Rearz on their website.)

That's because a baby pacifier's bulb will be much too small for an adult to stimulate the actual sensation a baby feels when they suck on their binky. By using a pacifier that has been sufficiently 'scaled up', so to speak, you'll both give your submissive the 'gagged' feeling of having a large rubber bulb stuck in their mouth, as well as effectively prevent them from making noise when they're not allowed.

65

PACIFIER FEEDER

I haven't found this product for sale anywhere yet, but a friend of mine who is a Dominant and a nurse is fond of this mechanism she custom made.

Her Little was being very naughty during their feeding sessions, and she decided she was through with him putting him with such a fuss.

So, what she did was strap him completely into his bed, then inserted and strapped a special large pacifier into his mouth that had a hole through its center.

Then, using a feeding tube, my friend dripped this submissive's breakfast mush through a feeding tube through his pacifier. The submissive was forced to eat the mush as it came, as every time he swallowed, his tongue compressed the bulb of the pacifier, pulling more mush into his mouth.

I wouldn't recommend this without the medical knowledge to do it safely, but I have to admit, watching my friend feed her humiliated, helpless Little in this way made me think it was the best method of feeding there was!

66

LEARNING TO CRAWL

Using clothing or other means to force your Little to crawl is a wonderful thing to watch.

Here are a few examples of how to force them to crawl:

1. Put your Little in a pair of locking PJ's that have their feet or legs sewn together.
2. Put ankle restraints around your Little that are bound so tight together they're touching. Your little will be able to choose between hopping or crawling on their knees. And if they try to hop, I promise they'll be on their knees soon enough.
3. Use special shoes that make walking impossible either through significant bulk below their feet, or if you're feeling extra cruel, a special pinching mechanism that makes it very painful for your Little to stand on them for any length.

I also know a domme to a sissy baby that straps extreme high heels on her baby that are so tall that they can't help but crawl. That's also a way to do it!

Another technique?

Spreader Bars.

A spreader bar is simply a bar strapped between someone's ankles or wrists that that prevents the wearer from closing their hands or legs.

Attaching a spreader bar to a submissive's ankles can be a fun way to make sure they crawl and don't go far.

But do you know what I like about it even more? That when you're putting the submissive on the diaper change table, you can easily grab and pull the bar up to get access to their bottom or privates.

You can even build a little hook that hangs from you ceiling above your change table that you can set the Little's spread bar on to keep their feet up while you change them. How useful!

67

WRAPPED IN PLASTER

Finally, I'll share one more tip from my nurse friend. She likes to take her submissive into her doctor's clinic after hours for a little 'custom' treatment.

This dominant will wrap both of the submissive's legs in a plaster or synthetic cast that will go all the way from the submissive's ankles up to around their waist. However, they leave the submissive's diapered groin freely visible.

By locking her submissive into such a cast, she has the excuse she needs to wheel her submissive around in a wheelchair, as the submissive is unable to walk and everyone understands this from the cast her legs are in.

But they also see the diaper her submissive is wearing with far less suspicion. After all, if her legs are broken and wrapped in casts, she certainly can't help herself to the bathroom very easily.

Not only does this make it much easier for this dominant to take her submissive out and about with their diaper showing, but it makes the Little dependent on her dominant in a real, more permanent way than anything else I've seen.

I don't have the expertise to pull such a thing off myself, but I have to admit, it sounds like fun!

PART VII
SISSIFICATION

Sissification, also known as 'feminization', is the act of turning a boy Little into a girl Little. While it's humiliating to be transformed from an adult into a baby, it can be similarly humiliating for a man to be transformed into a girl, especially if you know that said man foolishly prided themselves their masculinity as an adult.

While there are many guides you can look into that give you far more specifics about the details of sissy clothing and style, I wanted to give you the basics so you know that, should you wish to transform you submissive's gender, here are the basic details to doing so.

Just remember the key is that, they're your baby, so you get to decide what gender they are, not them!

SISSY CATALYSTS

The catalyst for Sissifying your baby can be anywhere from catching them looking at or trying on Mommy's dresses, to as simple as proclaiming how cute they look when you put them in a pink article of clothing.

It's helpful to declare, "Wow my little baby, I made the big mistake of thinking you were a little boy, when it's clear you're a little girl!"

You might slip a pink pacifier in your sissy baby's mouth and turn to your friend to proclaim, "Look at how cute she Looks? It's clear that pink is his color. Did I say 'his'? My mistake, I should have said *her* pacifier."

The key element is to proclaim to your new Sissy baby that you've discovered their *new* and *proper* gender. That they were *pretending* to be a boy, but now you've discovered that they are in fact an *adorable, pretty, sissy baby princess* at heart.

Also, you may find it more helpful to begin sissifying your Little *before* they become your diapered baby, thus reducing their defenses and getting them used to having you decide what humiliating articles of clothing to wear.

Alternatively, you may find it easier after you have already regressed them back to diapers, as they already know you make all their decisions for them.

It's up to you to find the path of regression and sissification that works best for you and your Little!

69

SISSY NAMES

If you've read the rest of the guide so far, you'll already know that you'll want to implement a baby name to take the place of your Little's previous adult name.

This is the same concept, except choose a girl's name instead of a boy's name. You can choose a totally new girl's name, or, I personally like to modify their previous name into a girly name. For example, George becomes Georgina or Carter becomes Catherine. That's because by retaining and transforming their old name, you're helping them make the *transition* into their new identity.

You can choose this new, 'sissy' name when you first decide their new baby name (just choose a sissy, baby name), or, you can give them a baby name at first, and decide to sissify them with a girlish version of their baby name later on when you wish to take the step of 'sissifying them'.

70

SISSY WARDROBE

For a sissy, the most important part of their transformation will be the clothing you put them in. Of course, you can start with pink or otherwise girlish diapers.

Then you can move on to filling their closet with new sissy pink onesies, PJs, and plastic bloomers. You'll want lots of pink and girly pacifiers. And of course, for anytime they leave the house, they'll need adorable pink dresses, rompers and pink fluffy tutus.

You'll want to take special time washing, brushing, and doing your sissy Little's hair every morning, making it long and girly and beautiful. Or, if they don't have long enough hair, you can shave their head and buy them an adorable wig of flowing, shiny blonde locks for them to wear at all times.

You'll also want to do their makeup, giving them adorable, sissy baby pink cheeks, long eye lashes, and bright red lipstick.

Do you know what my favorite part is of putting a Sissy Little in an adorable skirt or dress? It's so much easier to check their diaper! All you have to do when, say, waiting in the check-out line in the grocery store, is grab their skirt is lift it all the way up, so everyone else can see their diapered bottom, then give it a nice pat and a sniff!

71

INSIDE THE DIAPER

Lastly, when sissifying your Little, you'll make it clear to the Little at every opportunity, such as during a diaper change, that they no longer have a peepee. What they now have is an itty bitty clitty. And when you clean and wipe their 'itty bitty clitty,' make sure you coo in their ear how they're being such a 'good girl' letting Mommy clean their 'Itty bitty Clitty.'

And for the final touch, you should equip yourself with a large, penis shaped dildo, and ram it into your Little Sissy's bottom as often as possible. Tell them they're being a 'good girl' for 'taking your cock' like all little Sissies love to do. Soon your Sissy Little will love taking your cock, almost as much as their diapers, and their transformation will be complete.

How cute!

PART VIII
SEX

The best part about having an adult baby in the house is that, as your baby, you can experience all the joy of the many ways discussed above of taking complete control over your little one.

But as an adult, your submissive Little is a sexual being. While this can unfortunately lead to naughty behavior that you must always be on the lookout for (masturbation is covered in full below), it also means you can experience the incredible thrill and joy of having absolute sexual power over them. You can even, if you wish, have them satisfy you sexually in whatever way you please.

Personally, the best orgasms of my life have come from naughty boys eating my pussy while locked in soggy diapers. If you haven't experienced that thrill yourself yet, I certainly can't recommend it enough.

72

BOTTOM INSPECTIONS

While I considered starting this section off with the topic of masturbation (Masturbation is the number one offense most Little's commit according to most dommes I talk to), I find this first topic of bottom stroking to be even more... penetrating.

That's because for me, as a domme, one of the most exciting aspects of changing my Little's diaper is the opportunity I get to stick my long finger deep into their bottom while they're on the diaper changing table.

Nothing compares to the look on their face as I slowly maneuver my gloved digit to their exposed, puckering rose bud. Then, feeling for the entrance, I'll slowly push my long index finger into their tight bottom hole. I love to feel the resistance of them trying to squeeze my finger out of their bottom like it was some sort of intruder. I then love to watch their face as they stare at the ceiling and gasp as I push my digit past their resistance, feeling deep inside their bottom where they never thought it was possible for someone else to go.

I'll then wiggle my finger around inside of them, doing a careful inspection inside of them while they helplessly wait at my mercy.

My first goal is to thoroughly check the status of their colon so I know whether or not they need to poop (and if I should give them some help in the form of glycerin suppositories.)

But my second, and equally important reason for doing this every diaper change is that I want my Little to know that I am in charge of every corner of their body. They themselves will have never felt up their own bottom, yet here I am, twisting my digit inside them like a finger puppet, letting them know that they belong to me in every way possible.

I finger my Little's every diaper change, whether they're wet, or messy, or totally dry. First, because I relish the feeling of power that comes from the act.

And second, I know that by performing this action every single time my little is on their diaper change table, the Little forms the association of getting clean with my fingers in their bottom. I want them to internalize the sensation and expect it multiple times a day. I want them to always walk around with the faint feeling of my fingers in their bottom.

Depending on what mood I'm in, I'll then slip my digit out and watch my Little exhale as I do so. Then, I'll dip my index finger and middle finger into a large gob of Vaseline. Then I'll stretch my Little's anus out as I push those two fingers deep inside of them again.

I'll listen to them whimper and watch them squirm as I stretch out their bottom, twisting and spreading my fingers, working to open their anus as much as possible, despite their involuntary resistance.

If their colon is full, I'll open and close my fingers like scissors, stimulating their impending bowel movement. And as I stretch their anus open more every diaper change, I know I make it harder and harder for them to have any control over when they void their bowels at all.

Sometimes I'll even put a third digit into my Little as I put a Paci in their mouth to bite on. And sometimes I'll tell my little to try and expel my fingers, "Like you're doing a poopy," just to feel the sensation of them trying their hardest and failing to push me out.

And when I'm done, I always leave my Little's anus feeling strangely tingly and satisfied.

That's because my Little's know that I love them very much, and every time I change their diapers, I show that to them with my fingers. And I encourage you, as a domme, to do the same.

73

MASTURBATION

Whether you want it to or not, your Little's Masturbation habits will soon become a reality you must face head on.

That's because, in the first place, the fact that your Little is now locked in diapers and under your control will mean they no longer will be taking part in any sexual activity with other individuals.

This is for the obvious reason that they likely won't be leaving your eye sight, let alone your house, now that they're your full time Little. And if they did, the fact that they're now totally diaper dependent makes them utterly unattractive to the vast majority of sexual partners they may have desired in the past.

This is all excellent and exciting for you as the full time dominant over your submissive, because it means in addition to controlling everything from the food they eat to when they use their diapers, you also get to control whether or not you want your submissive to experience any sexual activity, and if so what and how that activity is.

Controlling your submissive's basic sexual needs in this way is a tool just as powerful as controlling their potty needs. For example, some would say that removing your Little's ability to ever have an orgasm again is just as significant, if not more significant, than removing their ability to ever have a bowel movement in private again.

But to return to the topic at hand, for Little's with penises, I guarantee you that as soon as you transition your submissive to diapers and start changing their diapers in the morning, you'll begin to find 'mysterious stains' in the front of their diaper (I'm talking about semen stains.)

That's for the basic reason that even if your submissive was in the habit, before they were diapered, of masturbating in the shower, in the bathroom, or even fastidiously cleaning up when they were finished masturbating in their bed, they will now no longer have that option. Therefore, they will start masturbating and orgasming in their diapers.

Personally, I find the masturbation habits of boys to be highly detestable and offensive in general. To me, it's telling that most boys are so cravenly enslaved to their naughty, self-indulgent, reckless masturbation habits, they won't think twice about sticking their hand into their diaper filled with urine, even feces, to start 'jerking one out', totally undeterred by their unsanitary state.

(I encourage you to see this for yourself by investing in a black light and using it to do a 'thorough inspection' during your Little's diaper change every morning. Even if you watch the Little make a poopy mess into a clean diaper you just put them in, and then you put the Little to bed in that poopy diaper, I guarantee you'll find that they didn't let that stop them from 'choking the chicken' overnight, as evidenced by the cum stain you'll still find in their diaper in the morning.)

In general, I find this indulgent behavior of Littles of any gender giving themselves an orgasm to be dirty, shameful, and not appropriate for a babyish, diapered Little.

Therefore, I encourage you to put a stop to your submissive's masturbation habits at once by all means at your disposal.

Firstly, I encourage you to do the above suggestion, and start silently observing and recording your Little's 'special messes' with a black light during their diaper changes.

Then, when you feel the time is right, you should 'bust' your Little for their naughty habit by pointing out the stain in their diaper. The more shame, humiliation and disgust you can heap on your Little for 'playing with themselves' the better.

You should issue a firm punishment to your Little for their naughty habit. Personally, I enjoy issuing a painful and humiliating spanking. If it's possible, try to shame your Little as much as possible for their 'dirty habit' by say, calling up your relatives and have your Little listen to the phone calls as you tell them how 'disappointed' you are.

That being said, don't institute the bondage methods discussed above yet to prevent masturbation! Instead, put your Little to bed in their crib in the same way that you did before, 'letting' them masturbate, so to speak.

Then, in the morning, you can discover their naughtiness and issue an even harsher punishment. For example, you can double their spanking.

You should repeat this cycle for some time, giving the Little the space they need to shame themselves, and then punishing them for it every morning.

Why? Firstly, it creates a strong link in the Little's mind between shame, orgasms, punishment and pleasure and pain. By transforming their sexuality into one that becomes intimately linked and determined by diapers and your punishments, you'll be working to psychologically regress them on a deep, subconscious, psycho-sexual level.

Secondly, the experience you've now created will put the submissive into a torturous situation every night by their own doing. That's because they will be internally battling both the shame of their masturbation habit and fear of your punishment, with the intense sexual urges that they won't be able to control.

When your submissive gives in and plunges their hand into their diaper every night, they'll be molding their sexuality into a new dependence on diapers. And when they orgasm, they'll be hit with waves of shame, not only about the fact that they masturbated at all, but that they were so craven they were willing to masturbate in wet and dirty diapers.

I would let this cycle of masturbation and punishment continue for about two weeks, progressively increasing the severity of your punishment. Know that even if your submissive has a 'clean' diaper one morning, that they still likely struggled all night with their filthy urges.

Finally, when you think that you've made a strong enough impact on your submissive, I would wait to 'catch them in the act'. This will be easy if you watch them in their crib on a nanny cam that you install.

When you catch them with their 'hand in their diaper', so to speak, make sure to pull them out of bed and heap intense amount of shame on them. Then I recommend you immediately implement one of the many restraining methods used above (such as locking plastic pants or bulky mittens) to put them back to bed, knowing they'll never be performing such a filthy act again in your house.

As they roll around and whine and cry about no longer having access to their 'filthy toy', as I like to call it, they'll probably resort to humping the bed or rubbing their crotch with their padded mitts.

Don't worry, orgasm through these means is highly difficult, and will only result in a deep psychological frustration on behalf of your submissive as they internalize the new level of total and utter control you know possess over their life.

And if they do manage to orgasm in their wet diaper simply by humping it, consider it a victory. It'll be crystal clear they now love their diapers more than you ever could have hoped for.

74

MASTURBATION PART II
THE 'FINISH THE WHOLE PACK' METHOD

Here is an alternative method of curing masturbation that I've discovered that you might enjoy.

It came to me as I remembered once when I was caught smoking cigarettes by my father as a young girl. Instead of giving me a lecture and taking the cigarettes away, my father implemented an alternative, much more effective punishment. He demanded I smoke the whole pack of cigarettes, right then and there. Ten Cigarettes later, after I was done wheezing and throwing up, I knew I would never touch another cigarette again.

Similarly, when I caught one of my Little's once with their hand plunged deep into their poopy diaper, furiously masturbating in their crib, I gave my Little a new rule.

The new rule, I told him, was that since he loved masturbating in his poopy diaper so much, that I would never change his diaper until he masturbated in them.

At first, he was delighted, as this Little already become aroused by the idea of diapers, and he loved to play with himself in them.

However, when we were out the next day, hanging out with my friends in the small back yard behind their house, the laxatives I put in his morning milk made him make a really big poopy mess in his diaper in front of everyone, which he found humiliating enough. So, he was suddenly no longer thrilled when I told him that he would either have to masturbate to orgasm in front of everyone in his poopy diaper, or he could stay in it all evening.

Or, the next night, when his poor little weewee was so tired from orgasming for three diaper changes that day, he couldn't orgasm no matter how hard he tried that night, so he was sent to bed in a messy diaper.

And you can imagine, one week later, how much he preferred to wade around in his stinky diapers then masturbate again for a change.

Now my Little regards his filthy little pecker as a source of deep and enduring humiliation, an unfortunate and lasting burden of his diapered life. Just the way I like it.

75

EDGING

While my last story may have sounded cruel, I think the cruelest I've behaved is towards Little's who have had their ability to masturbate completely taken away from them (by being restrained with the necessary clothes), yet who, every diaper change, I've adopted the unique and thrilling sport of masturbating them right up until the point where they might orgasm, and then stopping.

Why have I started doing this? Well for one, I love the look on their faces while I tug their hard, tall-standing, little pecker while they're hands and legs are bound and a soiled diaper is right at their bottom. I love the way their tongue comes out, their eyes cross, or they whimper and whine through their pacifier as I tug at their 'little guy'.

And then, as I sense the telltale motion in their testicles that suggests they're seconds away (an acquired skill), I love stopping cold turkey, and hearing them whimper and whine as I pull my hand away.

I usually like to tell them it's their fault, that they couldn't come fast enough for an orgasm, or I'll tell them maybe they'll get an orgasm next diaper change if they're good.

I love the way this game of mine changes their view of diaper changes. I love that whenever I tell them it's time for a diaper change, they leap into my arms with puppy dog excitement and run to be strapped onto the diaper change table, desperate for more of Nanny's "special massage".

And every once in a blue moon, I'll fail my mission, and they'll blow semen out of the top of their pecker in the epic orgasm they've been praying for for months. I'll pat their head, tell them that they're such a dirty little boy in a sweet voice, clean them up, and then begin the process of building up their urge again by time they have their next diaper change.

So, can you see now why I find this technique so fun?

76

CHASTITY

If you find that your Little is figuring out how to have orgasms despite the bondage and monitoring mechanisms you institute to prevent it, you may find it easier just to go the route of putting their penis or vagina in a standard chastity device.

Locking devices for all genitalia are now very easy to buy online and apply to your submissive and fit well under any diapers.

Some domme's find a chastity device to be a merciful alternative to some of my anti-masturbation methods I described above, as they prevent Little's with penises from getting an erection altogether, which would normally trap them in a state of unsatisfiable arousal. (What can I say, I'm not so nice.)

Also, if you have a Sissy Little, you may find that chastity better transforms their penis into the 'itty bitty clitty' you now see it as. Further, with this way, if you wish to give your Sissy any orgasm at all, you can only make those orgasms through insertion (prostate massage.)

Speaking of which...

77

PROSTATE MASSAGE

The prostate is a gland in males that can be accessed by reaching a finger or toy into their anus. A skilled dominant can actually cause their submissive to have a prostate-orgasm even while their Little is in chastity.

This can be a useful technique to you if you're raising a Sissy (discussed above), or if you want drain your submissive's balls in a way that doesn't allow them to feel their naughty little pecker being stroked. Being 'milked' in this way can be highly humiliating in of itself for the submissive, and might make a wonderful addition to your arsenal.

For example, let's say that you have the rare submissive who detests their diapers so much that will not bring themselves to have an orgasm or feel aroused in their diapers even if you demand it.

Imagine how humiliating it will be for them when you secure them face down on their diaper change table, and force them to have an orgasm in their wet diaper by using their 'rear entrance.'

Here are the simple steps to a prostate massage:

1. Apply a generous amount of lube to both the toy and the submissive's butt hole.
2. Then gently nudge the stimulator or your finger into their rectum. If using a toy, it should be anatomically designed to hit all the right spots.
3. If you're having trouble fitting a toy into your submissive's bottom, feel free to use your fingers to 'loosen them up.'
4. Tell your submissive to begin contracting and releasing their groin muscles. The way to explain this to them is to first tell them to try and go pee, then to contract like they're trying to stop their stream of urine.
5. Here's what's happening when they do this exercise: the rectal wall muscles are slightly drawing the toy in and out, causing it to bump against the prostate. The harder you contract, the harder it bumps. This is what leads to climax.
6. Finally, here are the five steps you can expect for your submissive to experience up until their orgasm:

1. Stimulation
2. Contractions
3. Buildup
4. Trembling
5. Orgasm

When they finally achieve orgasm, you'll see milky cum poor out of their penis, even if it's flaccid!

Yay!

Here's a bonus! You know that special milk you forced your submissive to produce with their orgasm?

Here's a tip. Collect it in a jar. Then, next time you prepare their milk bottle, add their 'special milk' into the bottle and swirl it around.

When you give them their milk bottle to drink, let them get about half way through, then gently ask them, "Hi little baby, does your milk taste funny at all?" And whether they say yes or no, you can then tell them with a smile that it's because they're drinking *their own* milk this time.

The look on their face will be priceless.

VIBRATORS

A prostate vibrator is an extremely useful tool if seeking to use the prostate orgasm method described above.

But a more standard vibrator is also a great toy to have. I recommend a 'magic wand' style vibrator, as this will be large and broad enough to send its vibrations through a diaper you hold it up to.

If you have a Little with a vagina, using a vibrator can be a fantastic method of either inducing orgasm in their diaper or edging (both of which I described more above.)

I know one domme with a female Little she loves very much. She knows her Little hates being in poopy diapers, so her favorite activity is holding a vibrator up to the crotch of her Little's diaper after she's made a stinky. She loves watching her Little writhe in the unique mixture of pleasure and disgust at being uncontrollably stimulated to orgasm in such a humiliating state.

I also know other domme's who use a vibrator on the outside of their bound-up boy-Little's, as the intense vibrations are capable of triggering a traditional orgasm via their erection, especially if they haven't been allowed to masturbate in a long time. The best part about that is that all their cummies is contained in their diaper and they didn't have to put their hands anywhere icky!

PEGGING

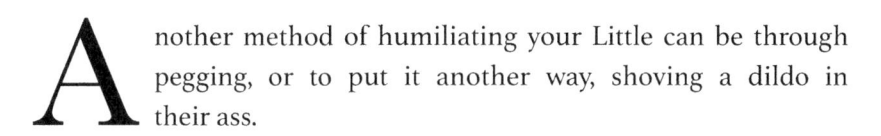

Another method of humiliating your Little can be through pegging, or to put it another way, shoving a dildo in their ass.

While I covered this in the 'sissy' section before, I think it's worth keeping in mind that shoving the huge shaft of a dildo in your submissive's ass during a diaper change is always a great way to remind them who is in charge.

Or, if you'd like to be even more intimate with it, you can strap the dildo on your crotch with a 'strap on' device, and climb on them, pull their diaper off, and fuck them in the ass to remind them of the little sissy baby they are.

TEACHING LITTLE'S HOW TO GIVE

While all of the above has focused on the sexuality and orgasms of your submissives (an undeniably important topic), we dominants shouldn't forget whose orgasms matter the most — ours.

Whether you choose to have your submissive give you an orgasm, or you simply masturbate in private after you've 'put them down' for the night, I can't encourage you enough to take the pleasure you deserve as a hard-working caretaker of your little!

My personal favorite method of orgasm is the 'climax for a change' method. That is, I institute a rule with my Little that in order for them to get a diaper change before I put them to bed, they must eat my pussy until I orgasm.

When my Little was starting out eating my pussy at night, they were very unskilled with their mouth and tongue, and typically after about thirty minutes of them failing miserably at their task, I would put them to bed in their soggy diapers.

However, after a few nights of spending their whole night in a messy diaper, my Little started to become quite a bit better with their tongue.

Now I don't even have to ask. By around 7:30pm, my Little is begging for me to take my pants off so they can start eating 'Mommy's Pussy Cream Pie.'

What a good Little I have!

81

CUCKOLDING

As an alternative to having your Little give you sexual pleasure, it's a totally reasonable and wonderful choice to instead fuck other, real men and women after you put your Little to bed!

This is a great choice for women who are diaper regressing their former boyfriend or husband because they found them to be disappointing partners or lovers.

After you experience the joy of regressing your former spouse to a babyish, diaper-dominated state, you can now enjoy the pleasure of fucking all the other men in the world who are begging to be with you.

And now, when you invite a man over to fuck you however you like to be fucked, you can introduce them to your 'little baby,' adding to your submissive's utter humiliation.

And when you orgasm that night in your new man's arms, you can multiply your delight knowing that every second of pleasure you experience with your new man inherently increases the helpless and humiliation your submissive Little feels while they're bound up and diapered in their crib.

Want another tip? Reverse your Little's nanny Cam, so they get to watch on screen as their new 'mommy' fucks someone else. Or better yet, roll their crib into your bedroom so they can watch the whole thing happen before their eyes while the suck their little Paci and cry.

PART IX

FORCED INCONTINENCE & ADVANCED DIAPER USAGE

At this point in the guide, you've learned how to regress your submissive and keep them in their diapers, whether they want to wear them or not.

However, sometimes a dominant needs more tools in her tool belt when it comes to forcing her submissive to really 'embrace' their new diapered status.

I encourage you to read up on the following tools, some of which you may need to employ on a routine basis (such as glycerin suppositories for a Little who resists making poopy diapers) or for very special occasions (like a catheter).

The important thing is that you, as a domme, have the tools you need to take total control over your submissive in the way that matters most — ensuring they use their diapers.

CATHETERS

Catheters come with a much higher risk and difficulty level than any of the other methods below. I don't recommend using them without the help of a medical professional.

(My friend, who is a nurse, is a big fan of using catheters on her Little, but she knows what she's doing, and says that if you don't know what you're doing, you run the risk of exposing your Little to serious infection. So be careful!!)

That being said, I wanted to include them first as they're the only method to induce loss of bladder control (as opposed to loss of bowel control like the rest of the methods below.)

The solution? Schedule your Little a visit to a nurse or doctor who understands their diapered condition. Let them put a catheter in while you still get the fun of changing your Little's diapers.

Here are the steps involved, if only so you can understand the process a medical professional will through:

1. If male, hold the penis with the non-dominant hand. Maintain hand position until preparing to inflate balloon.

2. Using dominant hand to handle forceps, cleanse peri-urethral mucosa with cleansing solution. Cleanse anterior to posterior, inner to outer, one swipe per swab, discard swab away from sterile field.
3. Pick up the catheter with gloved (and still sterile) dominant hand. Hold end of catheter loosely coiled in palm of dominant hand.
4. In the male, lift the penis to a position perpendicular to patient's body and apply light upward traction (with non-dominant hand)
5. Identify the urinary meatus and gently insert until 1 to 2 inches beyond where urine is noted
6. Inflate balloon, using correct amount of sterile liquid
7. Gently pull catheter until inflation balloon is snug against bladder neck
8. Connect catheter to drainage system (in this case it will drain into their diaper).

When your Little is wearing a catheter inserted by a professional, they will experience the sensation of truly losing bladder control as their pee drips into their diaper in a constant stream.

Doesn't that sound fun?

LAXATIVES - A PRIMER

For those that don't know by now, laxatives are defined broadly by their ability to cause urgent, possibly uncontrollable, bowel movements. Many types are available to be purchased over the counter at any drug store.

While it takes some work to create the circumstances for your submissive to begin wetting (peeing in) their diaper regularly (unless they're wearing a catheter, of course), it's much easier to cause them to involuntarily mess, even at early stages of their regression.

This is for two reasons. First, the bowels have only one sphincter, and it has to be much more flexible than the urethra's two sphincters. Second, the bowels handle everything that the body doesn't absorb, making it easy for many substances to induce their irritation.

There are four general types of laxatives worth keeping in mind.

1. Dietary Fiber/Bulk-Forming Laxatives

Examples: Bran, Ispaghula husk, Methylcellulose, Sterculia, Prunes, Bananas

These laxatives increase the size and liquidity of the bowel movement. These are good for long-term use, but might not produce a sudden or irresistible urge. Bulk-forming laxatives are great for general health, and may reduce the risk of colon cancer. However, they won't produce the immediate results that will be of most use to you when dealing with your submissive.

2. **Stimulant/ Irritant Laxatives**

Examples: Senna, Sodium picosulfate, Castor oil, Bisacodyl, Cascara, Docusate, Dantron, Docusate sodium

These laxatives irritate the bowel or increase the bowel's sensitivity. They can produce a strong urge, and possibly cramping, after about 5–12 hours. The initial firm movement may be followed by runny movements (so it might be worth putting your Little in plastic pants!) You'll also want them to be drinking plenty of liquids to avoid dehydration (which they should be doing anyway!)

Castor Oil, which I reference specifically above in the 'punishment' section, is a clear, viscous liquid, a little like peanut oil, but with an ominous aura that lingers on the palette. One can just feel it slowly worming it's way through the digestive tract, slithering through from end to the other.

Senna is an herbal laxative that is quite businesslike. It comes in brown, leafy pills as generic Senna, and small, sweet pills as "Ex-Lax." The pills take effect after several hours and produce multiple, soft movements. These movements are urgent, but can be fought for a short time. Depending on the dosage, there can be some cramping.

3. **Lubricant**

Examples: Mineral Oil, Flaxseed oil, Olive oil

These lubricate the rectum, increasing urgency while reducing one's ability to resist.

4. **Osmotic/Hypersomotics**

Examples: Magnesium salts, Glycerol (Glycerin) suppositories, Lactitol, Lactulose, Macrogols

These laxatives prevent the extraction of water from feces, and may draw more water into the bowels. They literally flush out the system. They may produce runny stools (so put those plastic pants on your Little!)

The salt-based (saline) laxatives may take effect in as little as one hour. The sugar-based (lactulose) work more slowly. Magnesium citrate is available in single-dose bottles. The solution tastes salty, as would be expected. You can slide this right into a warm milk solution.

Faster still are glycerin suppositories. They are direct, quick, and efficient, acting in around 15 minutes to an hour. The best part? You insert them into your Little rectally.

I highly recommend using glycerin suppositories as your primary method of forced bowel movements for you Little.

Further, this is also why I always advocate fingering your Little's bottom every diaper change. That way they won't know when you've inserted rectal suppositories or not, and their urgent and severe loss of control will be to their humiliating surprise!

84

ENEMAS

Enemas are a classic tool to induce incontinence, and in fact they're often a subject of fetish in of themselves! The difference is that often those who fetishize enemas but not diapers will let their submissive run to the toilet to release their bowels. I, on the other hand, will allow no such thing, and often enjoy both the process of giving an enema as well as the incredible mess that they make in a Little's diaper when they come out!

Here are the basic steps to giving an enema:

1. Gather the needed materials (enema bag or bulb, lubricant, gloves, enema solution, ramp clamp, and an extra diaper for leakage.)
2. Warm the solution before placing it into an enema bag or bulb to a temperature between 99 and 106 degrees.
3. Place a spare diaper under your Little to collect any leakage during the procedure.
4. Lay your Little on the diaper change table in a position to receive the enema. The ideal positions for enema administration are the right side position, left side position,

knee chest position, and on the back. It is advised that your Little remain in one of these positions to receive the enema for one-third of the time.

5. Lubricate the tip of the enema applicator before inserting it into the rectum of your Little. Ensure that the entire length of the enema tip is lubricated and that the opening of the tip remains free from clogs so that the solution flows freely when the time comes to administer the enema.
6. Insert the lubricated enema tip into your Little's rectum and release the enema tubing clamp.
7. Monitor your Little for cramping as the enema solutions flows comfortably into their rectum. Signs of cramping may include abdominal muscle tension.
8. If your Little starts cramping, and you wish to be merciful, you may stop the flow and ask them to take several deep breaths. You can continue the flow once the cramping subsides again.
9. Gently massage your Little's abdominal area. Massage down the left portion of their abdomen then massage from left to right across the lower belly button. Continue to massage up the right portion of the abdomen then massage from right to left under your Little's rib cage.
10. Remove the tip of the enema from your Little's rectum once the device is empty. Ask them to remain in the current position until he or she has a strong urge for a bowel movement.
11. Put your Little in a thick diaper and tell them to hold it for as long as possible.

If this is a punishment, now just put your Little in the corner and enjoy the show as they dance and squirm until they mess themselves!

HOLLOW BUTT PLUGS

Another technique I enjoy for inducing incontinence and humiliating accidents in my Littles is the use of a hollow butt plug.

A hollow butt plug is just like a normal butt plug, but it has a hole in the middle of it.

If your Little's stool is runny enough (see laxatives above), they will simply drip their poop into their diaper without even realizing it or having any way to stop it!

Imagine how humiliated they'll feel when you start sniffing the air, and then do a diaper check on them out of the blue. They they'll realize that their bottom is wet and full of warm mush, and they'll realized in horror they pooped themselves without even knowing!

One way to make the best use of hollow butt plugs is to make steady use of normal (non-hollow) butt plugs for your Little, which can be inserted during their diaper changes (more on that below).

Because your Little will have no idea when they're butt plug is solid or when it's hollow, it will only enhance their feeling of helplessness that they could have a poopy accident at any time!

ANAL STRETCHING

Another longer-term method of dominating your submissive and eliminating their bowel control is by anal stretching.

To put it simply, you can buy butt plugs and dildos in gradations of sizes that go from small to large in order to stretch them out.

The method I've used is the 'plugged' method. That is, during every diaper change, I insert a butt plug into my submissive. The feeling of being plugged a very all-encompassing feeling, and the feeling of being 'full' down there, combined with their diaper, will certainly have a transformative impact on your Little's overall behavior.

Then, as the days go by, slowly increase the width of their butt plugs. I tend to let my submissive sleep without a plug in (to give their anal muscles a chance to rest), and I tend to use a hollow butt plug for about half the day so they can do their 'number two.'

As you get bigger and bigger with the butt plugs, their anus will begin to stretch more and more. Soon, you'll notice a distinct effect that when you pull the butt plug out, that their anus stays 'gaping', so to speak, unable to close as it did before.

This is the change you're looking for. Now that you've reached the 'stretch width' you've desired for them, you can let them run around for a day without a plug in, and experience the sensation of being unable to hold their sphincter shut to prevent their poopy accidents anymore.

That being said, you should alternative days, making sure to still keep them stretched and plugged every other day, to keep them from regaining sphincter closing ability.

You can also use inflatable butt plugs for this purpose, as they are easier to insert and expand to greater and greater circumferences.

Alternatively, you may instead enjoy employing dildos for your submissive's stretching purposes as well. It's the same concept, except about five times a day (or every diaper change), use the largest, ridged dildo possible to stretch out your Little's anus while they lay down and take it in their bottom for about ten minutes. Like with the butt plugs, you're looking for an eventual 'gaping' quality.

Have fun!

87

CONSTIPATION

While the last thing I want is for my Little's to be constipated, sometimes, when I'm dealing with a Little who I wish to issue a 'unique' punishment to, I will *induce* constipation.

This is easy to do by simply giving the Little any typical anti-diarrhea medicine, as it will thicken and remove water from their stool and make passing their bowel movement very difficult.

Then, when the time is right, I will induce a bowel movement using some combination of laxatives described above. The sensation of passing the largest, messiest bowel movement in their life (due to holding it for days) is a fantastic and memorable sight in of itself.

Combine this with a public viewing party, where I invite all my friends to come over and watch the Little make 'the messiest diaper you've ever seen', along with a public changing afterward, is quite the experience, and quite fun!

88

THE BANANA TECHNIQUE

This technique is basically the process of putting bananas in the submissive's rectum, which they will then be forced to expel in a messy and humiliating way.

This technique has gained some traction in the ABDL community, as it allows the subject to experience the sensation of pushing a 'mess' out their bum, but the fact that they're bananas makes clean up easier and reduces the smell.

The reason why I think it's worth a dominant learning this technique is that it can be a fun and humiliating way to make your submissive 'mess' for you, no matter how many times they've 'already gone.'

Further, it can be fun to watch the look on your submissive's face as you make them feel like they have to go poop again, even after you just changed them out of their messy diaper!

First, assemble the following ingredients:

- Four bananas. Not too ripe, but not green either. Break them each in half.
- Four liquid fleet suppositories

Steps:

1. Place banana halves in a glass bowl and microwave them for 30 seconds to bring them closer to body temperature.
2. Empty two of the fleet liquid suppository applicators onto the banana halves. Make sure the tips of each are lightly lubricated.
3. Empty the other two applicators into the submissive's rectum.
4. Slip the banana halves tip-first into your Little's bottom, one at a time. This may take a couple of minutes. It is a wonderfully strange sensation for your Little, so no need to race through this.
5. The first banana will completely smush up. Push as much as you can in with your gloved hand. It's weird, but believe it or not, they start to go in easier and easier. By the 3rd or 4th half, they pop right in. This is why you start with 8 halves. By the last half, you're Little will feel incredibly full.
6. Tightly diaper your Little. You may also wish to include plastic pant.
7. Allow your Little to lay calmly for a few minutes.
8. Then, make your Little stand up, and take them into a scenario where they must try as hard as possible to avoid losing control and messing themselves. This could be in the middle of a part you're throwing, a walk through the mall, or an intimate and quiet meeting with them and their teacher.

During this experience, the Little will obviously feel incredibly full of very wet warm and heavy mush. And the quick-acting suppository will be screaming at the poor Little's bowels "Void. Void!"

They'll be able to act normal and semi-intelligently at first. But then, in about 90 seconds, they'll feel it building — a nasty wave of cramping.

Everything goes crazy again. They can't focus, they can't speak.

They'll think, "It's happening, oh my god, I can't hold it... but then it backs off again." It's like wave after wave of contraction. Each one gets slightly stronger. And each one forces the sphincter to dilate a tiny bit more. This can sometimes go on for 45 minutes or longer.

After 30 to 60 minutes, your Little will be totally immersed in this experience. This is a supremely controlling on your behalf, as you know own their whole existence at this point as they focus on trying not to mess.

Finally, at some point your Little's tired and quivering sphincter will surrender all hope, and they will involuntarily spread their legs as their diapers fill with a mass of warm, wet, steamy ooze.

But that's not it, in most cases, about 30 seconds after the pressure is relieved from the prostate gland, the sub's bladder will involuntarily empty as well.

This qualifies as an emotionally, mentally and physically intense experience, sure to leave any Little completely chagrined, humiliated and weakened. Most dommes who have tried this recipe have been utterly blown away that such an intense form of control and humiliation can be relatively easily orchestrated with common grocery store items.

Enjoy!

MARSHMALLOWS

Want another homemade laxative from the grocery section of the store?

The sugars and gelatin in common marshmallows can act as a powerful suppository similar to glycerin suppositories when inserted rectally.

That's right, you can stick ordinary marshmallows up your submissive's bottom to make them poop.

Here's How:

1. Freeze seven large Marshmallows.
2. Put your submissive on their diaper change table, and make sure you have extra diapers, lubricant and plastic pants ready!
3. Stretch and lubricate your submissive's anus out with your fingers. Then, when you're ready, insert the first marshmallow. It should actually go in pretty easy. The reason you freeze the marshmallows is so that they hold up upon insertion.

4. You submissive will actually begin to feel the marshmallow 'getting things moving' almost immediately after you insert it. Keep going, filling them with anywhere between 3 and 7 marshmallows.
5. Clean their sticky bottom and put them in their diaper.
6. After about 15 minutes, your Little will feel an uncontrollable urge to go. Make a game out of it and make sure to incentivize them to try and hold it as long as possible!
7. Enjoy the look of humiliation and helplessness as they make a huge, uncontrollably mess in their diaper.

Trust me, the marshmallow may smell sweet going in, but they certainly don't when they come out!

PART X
ENHANCED PUNISHMENT

Finally, there may come a time for you as a domme when you're dealing with a Little who isn't... responding... to the usual methods of discipline as outlined above.

Or, it may just be the case that as a domme, you want to have a full understanding of all the tools at your disposal, so that should the day come, you'll know exactly how to traverse any hurdle a potential submissive may offer.

Either way, I warn you that the following techniques are not for the faint of heart. But then again, I doubt you would have read this far if you were faint of heart to begin with.

Enjoy!

90

ICE

Is your Little being too shy to wet? Dropping a handful of ice cubes in the front of their diapers and sealing them in will probably teach them to use their diaper right quick. That's because the only way they'll be able to escape the freezing sensation is if they let a warm flow of pee escape into their diaper, melting the ice cubes.

I know one Dominant who swears by this method, and when training a new Little for incontinence, she drops four ice cubes down their diaper every three hours for seven days straight, "To they show me that they know how to drink and wet as much as possible."

Yikes! But I guess you can't argue with results!

Bonus: If you have a submissive who won't stop humping in their diaper, but you don't want to put them in chastity, some ice in their diaper every time you catch them being naughty will shrink that peepee right down!

91

DIAPER RASH

Most of your time as a caretaker will be spent trying to keep your baby from getting diaper rash.

But sometimes us caretakers are feeling under-appreciated, and we need to teach our Little's how to appreciate the service we do for them by changing their diapers.

If you leave your Little in a soaked or messy diaper for longer than a few hours, they'll start to develop a rash. The more they slosh their mess around and move in their diaper, the worse it will get.

I once put a Little into their crib for an early bedtime with four suppositories up their bottom after they hadn't gone number two in days. (They had decided to try to spite me by holding their BM's).

The sound I heard through the baby monitor as I listened to them mess uncontrollably in the crib they were locked in that night was music to my ears. And when I walked in the next morning, they made the mistake of asking for a diaper change.

To teach them a lesson, I kept them in that cold, soiled diaper all day as we went to dance class in the park. His diaper rash was making him wince and whine as he pranced about in his soiled diaper and tutu in the park.

Finally, when we got home, I gave him a swift spanking (an extra cruel sensation when experiencing diaper rash), an hour of corner and mouth in soap time, and then finally changed his poopy diaper.

It was fascinating to observe how the diaper rash had spread so severely all across his crotch and buttocks. He was whimpering and begging for me to make it stop hurting.

I put the cool diaper rash cram in my hand, and made him promise he would never ever ask for a diaper change again. My point being that what he was afraid of — being left in his stinky diaper — would only be the consequences of his asking to be changed.

He immediately agreed, and coo'd as I treated his rash with cool cream. Ever since that day he's been an angel baby, never rudely and inappropriately asking for a diaper change again. And any diaper rash he's had since has only been the slightest discomfort compared to the out of control and humiliating rash he was subjected to that day.

So, as you can see, diaper rash can be a submissive's worst enemy, or a domme's best friend.

DIAPER WITHDRAWAL

One time I had a Little who would not stop begging to be taken out of his diaper. The humiliation of it for him was so intense, that he said he would do whatever I wanted, so long as he didn't have to wear a diaper. "Anything is better than wearing a diaper," he pleaded and pleaded.

I took him at his word, and that night I gave him 3 spoons of castor oil after an extremely heavy dinner. Then I took him into his bedroom, shoved 6 suppositories up his rear end (without him knowing), and then, to his surprise and delight, took his diaper away, telling him I would heed to his demand.

I then wrapped him up tight in a straightjacket, put restraints on both of his ankles, bound a pacifier gag into his mouth, and locked him in his crib for what I knew would be a long night.

I decided to shut off the baby monitor that night. As much as I thought I might enjoy the moans of him squalling for escape, I wanted to be surprised by what I found in the morning.

And in the morning, when I finally went in to check on him twelve hours later, the smell coming from his crib was worse than anything

I'd ever smelled before (and I've changed lots of poopy diapers, let me tell you!)

The poor boy not only loosed his bowels and bladder all over his bedsheets and blankets, but in his effort to escape his disgusting mess, he ended up rolling around and spreading around and laying in his mess all night.

I remember he looked up at me with puppy dog eyes, both sickened and humiliated by his infantile behavior. "Please Mama. Please put me back in diapers," were all he could say to me.

And I did! And we've never had a problem since. So, as you can see, sometimes distance (and a filthy mess) really does make the heart grow fonder.

ITCHY DIAPERS

Sometimes, if a Little I'm sitting really starts to make my angry for any number of reasons, I'll restore to one of the cruelest tricks I have. Itching powder in the diaper.

Itching powder is worse than any diaper rash. It will quickly consume the Little, turning every sense on their body, every fiber in their being, into a desire to scratch at their bottom, which their diaper padding prevents.

What's even worse? I enjoy wrapping them in a very thick disposable, along with a very thick cloth diaper. I'll then slip them into locking PJs, put their hand in thickly padded mittens, and pacifier gag them.

Nothing compares to how adorable and hilarious it is to see such a baby rolling on the floor, jumping in the air, and wiggling their butt against every surface possible in a vain effort just to scratch their little heinie.

What a cute baby! I bet they won't be complaining about sitting still during story time any longer!

94

CHAFING VELCRO

Do you love the waddle of a thickly padded diapered Little? Do you wish your Little couldn't run so fast away from you? Do you want your Little to slow down, even when they crawl?

Next time when you change them into their diaper, stick the rougher side of a piece of velcro to the crotch of their diaper, facing outward toward your Little's thighs.

Now, when your Little walks around, they'll be subject to an intense chafing anytime they walk. When they add urine to their diaper, the acidic urine will only make it burn worse.

Time to waddle like a good little baby!

95

CLOTHESPINS

If, for some reason, you need to make diaper changes for your submissive exponentially more unpleasant, you can make a habit of attaching clothespins to your submissive's nipples every time you lay them down and strap them to their diaper change table.

The fun thing about clothes pins is that they're iterative as well. You can, for example, add a clothespin for every transgression your Little committed that day. Just keep finding spots on your submissive's body to clip them to, such as their arms, thighs and lips.

If you want to enhance the psychological torment, clip the clothespins when they're not in use right on the rails of the diaper changing table as a constant visual reminder. Or better yet — clip them to the collar of your shirt so your Little know they're always one reach away from having an ouchie clothespin attached to them if they misbehave.

I know one domme who was purposefully peed on by a rebellious Little while they were on the diaper changing table. A clothes pin placed on his penis every diaper change after that soon made him regret that move!

I know another domme who used clothespins religiously with all the Little's she changes. I asked her why, and she said she wanted to make diaper changes inherently unpleasant for her Little's. She just loved dynamic of always having to find her stinky Little's when they needed a diaper change because they always want to put their diaper change off as long as possible. She liked that her Little's were acting like real babies in that way.

What a cute idea.

96

SPICY FOODS

Does your Little complain about the menu at your house, no matter what punishment you give them?

Since they're so insistent on 'big kid' food, I recommend you introduce them to a heaping pile of habanero peppers mixed into their dinner tonight.

If they were crying about their dinner before, they'll certainly be crying now as the extremely spicy food burns their mouth with bite after bite.

As an added bonus, if they were ever hesitant to drink their milk bottle before, they'll be thirstily chugging momma's milk down now in an effort to cool the spiciness.

The best part? The habanero peppers burn just as much on their way *out* of your Little as on their way *in*. Be prepared for some very hot, stinky bottoms in the near future!

THE 'TIME-OUT' PILLORY

I've included the 'time-out' pillory in this section, not because it's especially crueller than the corner time described above, but because aesthetically, it's inherently quite intimidating and medieval looking.

If you don't know, a pillory is a large board with three holes for securing the head and hands that was formerly used for punishment by public humiliation in earlier eras.

The pillory I built for my personal nursery is in fact bright white with pink and blue butterflies and pacifiers on it. I find the contrast between the device's purpose and its aesthetic to be quite pleasing.

To use the pillory is simple. Just walk your submissive over to the pillory, stick their head and hands in, and lock 'em in until further notice. Such a position is perfect for accessible spankings, or anything else you would like to do with their defenseless hiney.

My domme friend swears by the device for giving enemas. Her favorite method is to put the submissive into the pillory and start the flow of water. If it's the submissive's first time receiving such a punishment, they'll probably use a 'naughty word.

The domme will then get a bar of soap and shove it in the submissive's mouth, turning an unpleasant enema into an even more humiliating experience.

I believe she then leaves them to spill their enemas in their diaper, and finishes it off with a long spanking on top of their mess.

As you can see, the pillory makes all the work of an extensive punishment like that much easier. Well for the domme, anyway!

98

DILDO STOOL

The dildo stool is a small, three-legged stool that is so short it requires the submissive to squat when they wish to sit upon it.

But to sit on the stool, the submissive must have their diaper lowered by their caretaker. You might have guessed why. That's because out of the middle of the stool sticks a large, 6 inch dildo.

I've never owned one myself, but I once watched a Dominant send her Little to 'Time-out'. The Little's lip quivered when they heard their sentence and immediately grabbed their bottom in terror. I understood why when they walked to the closet a few seconds later with their domme, and a dildo stool was placed on the floor.

I watched as the submissive carefully lowered their bottom onto the thick, ridged dildo, doing their best to squat slowly enough to make the intrusion bearable.

The domme, fed up with how slow the submissive was going, then took it upon herself to pull the submissive's hand out from under them, causing them to collapse straight down into the giant dildo and yelp in pain and humiliation.

I admit, I enjoyed watching that cute submissive Little squat on their dildo stool for the next hour, cheeks as rosy as a cherry pie.

And when the submissive finally was able to leave time out, I watched the dildo slide out, and leave their anus still gaping open as they walked with their domme upstairs. Good thing they were wearing diapers!

FIGGING

This one might be one of the cruellest punishments on the list.

Figging is the practice of inserting a piece of skinned ginger root into the anus in order to generate an acute burning sensation. Historically it was a method of cruel corporal punishment, and well, the same can be said for today!

Here are the steps:

1. Buy a piece of ginger from the store, and skin it and carve it into the shape of a butt plug.
2. Insert the ginger into the submissive's anus and hold it there. Within seconds it will produce an intense burning sensation for the submissive, often reaching the level of intolerable discomfort.
3. The effect will reach climax within two to five minutes after insertion, and persists for around thirty minutes before gradually easing.
4. If you wish to extend a figging session, say because your submissive continued to be naughty or disrespectful during

it, you can further skin the same piece of ginger and reinsert it, extending the experience. Each fresh application of ginger root refreshes the duration of the sensations in the subject.

The cruellest part of this punishment? If the Little who is being figged tightens the muscles of their anus, the sensation becomes more intense.

I think there's a way here to teach naughty submissive's not to clench their butt to prevent BM's, but I haven't figured it out yet...

100

A WHIFF OF THEIR OWN MEDICINE

This one is easy but strikingly effective. I often use it for 'inappropriate language' on the diaper change table. ("Like Nanny, don't touch me down there!")

From now on, as you pull your submissive's used, wet diaper off, instead of putting it in their diaper pail, wrap it around their face.

Force them to smell the intense odor of their own urine mixed with the sweet smell of their diaper anytime they get changed. It's a deeply humiliating act for the submissive to say the least.

But be careful, it may backfire. One of my submissives, after I started doing this to him, grew to like the smell of his own diapers. I soon watched his peepee stand hard on end whenever I wrapped his used diaper around his face.

I didn't know what to do at that point, besides shrug and see it as a sign of his successful regression. I don't think he'll ever want to be taken out of diapers again!

101

THE REVERSE DIAPER CHANGE

I don't resort to this one often, but sometimes a submissive's attitude starts to rub me the wrong way, and I sense they're taking their diaper changes for granted.

The solution? Next time you put them on the table for a diaper change, instead of taking them out of their current messy diaper, just pull out a used diaper from their diaper change from the day before and tape it over their current diaper.

They'll likely be extremely confused, in which case you can explain, "You said you needed a diaper change, you didn't specify you wanted to be changed out of your *old* diaper and into a *new* diaper. So I'm just putting an old diaper on you!"

For extra comedy, keep taking them for 'diaper changes,' only to just keep adding used diapers.

Soon they'll hardly be able to walk (or breathe with the stench around their waist.) Yucky but fun!

Finally, I once heard of a domme who didn't have any toilets in the house she lived in with her Little.

When I heard this, I was confused, and asked the obvious follow up question — where did the domme go to the bathroom?

"They used their Little's diaper," they replied.

Surprised, I asked, "They wore diapers as well?"

"No, used their Little's Diapers," they replied.

"Oh, so they put a diaper on every time they needed to use the bathroom?" I asked again.

"*No*. They used their Little's diaper," they replied again.

I then finally understood. This Dominant was fed up with her Little sneaking into their house's bathroom when she wasn't watching. Her solution was to get rid of all the toilets altogether.

And from then on, when she needed to pee, she told her Little to sit on the floor and hold the front of their diaper open. The domme then released her bladder into their Little's diaper… while they were still wearing it.

I shudder to think how that dominant went… "Number Two" in that house. I didn't ask.

I warned you that this last section wasn't for the faint of heart!

IN CONCLUSION

Thank you for taking the time to get to the end of this guide! I hope reading about all the techniques I've used for diaper domination has inspired you take them and make them your own as you go on your own quest of having fun with your Little.

As always, be safe! Have fun! And enjoy all the gifts diaper punishment and domination has to offer!

XOXO

Nanny Chloe

MORE FROM NANNY CHLOE

Thank you for downloading and reading my little! To read Nanny Chloe's other work, please visit:

All My Stories:

https://nannychloe.weebly.com/

My Amazon Author Page:

http://www.amazon.com/author/nannychloe

Follow me on Tumblr and stay in touch!

http://nannychloetales.tumblr.com/

As always, your reviews and feedback are greatly appreciated, as they let Nanny Chloe know what you want to read in your ABDL stories. :)

Printed in Dunstable, United Kingdom